COLDHEARTED 3

No Loose Endz

LOU GARDEN PRICE SR.

URBAN AINT DEAD

Lou Garden Price, Sr.

100 BRIAR AVE

ROCHESTER, NH 03867

Contact Publisher at www.urbanaintdead.com

Email: urbanaintdead@gmail.com

Print ISBN: 979-8-9906748-5-1

CONTENTS

STAY UP TO DATE

To stay up to date on new releases, plus get information on
contests, sneak peaks and more,
Click the link below...
https://mailchi.mp/6d21003686d1/subscribe

<u>**Soundtracks**</u>

Scan the QR Code below to listen to the Soundtracks/Singles of some of your favorite U.A.D titles:

Don't have Spotify or Apple Music?
No Sweat!
Visit your choice streaming platform and search URBAN AINT DEAD.

Currently on lock serving a bid?
JPay, iHeartRadio, WHATEVER!
We got you covered.

Simply log into your facility's kiosk or tablet, go to music and search URBAN AINT DEAD.

URBAN AINT DEAD

Like & Follow us on social media:
FB - URBAN AINT DEAD
IG: @urbanaintdead
Tik Tok - @urbanaintdead

<u>**Submissions**</u>

Submit the first three chapters of your completed manuscript to <u>urbanaintdead@gmail.com</u>, subject line: Your book's title. The manuscript must be in a .doc file and sent as an attachment. The document should be in Times New Roman, double-spaced, and in size 12 font. Also, provide your synopsis and full contact information. If sending multiple submissions, they must each be in a separate email. Have a story but no way to submit it electronically? You can still submit to URBAN AINT DEAD. Send in the first three chapters, written or typed, of your completed manuscript to:

URBAN AINT DEAD
P.O Box 448
Maybrook, NY 12543

DO NOT send original manuscript. Must be a duplicate.
Provide your synopsis and a cover letter containing your full contact information.
Thanks for considering URBAN AINT DEAD.

ACKNOWLEDGMENTS

Thanks to the Lord Jesus Christ.

Blessings to all who purchased, read, rated, reviewed online (including ebook/kindle readers in the USA and outside) all my other novels:

Hittaz: Get It Back In Blood (Urbanaintdead.com) (Amazon/Kindle)

Hittaz 2: Real Killaz Don't Miss (Urbanaintdead.com) (Amazon/Kindle)

Hittaz 3: Contract Killaz (Urbanaintdead.com) (Amazon/Kindle)

Hittaz 4: As Grimey As It Gets (Urbanaintdead.com) (Amazon/Kindle)

Hittaz 5: Everybody Suspect (Urbanaintdead.com) (Amazon)

Coldhearted: Blood Stains & Broken Trust (Urbanaintdead.com) (Amazon)

Coldhearted 2: Rise Of A Street Tyrant (Urbanaintdead.com) (Amazon)

SosaFromScarface: The Saga Begins (Amazon/Kindle Direct Publishing)

Sosa: The Price of Power (Book One) (thecellblock.net) (Amazon)

Sosa 2: The Reign (thecellblock.net) (Amazon)

Sosa: Killing Tony Montana (Prequel) (thecellblock.net) (Amazon)

I'm thankful for the inquiries from everyone on what I'm doing or planning next. From my circle and readers. Well, they don't call me *The World's Monumental Storyteller* for nothing.

Hittaz 6: Chapter AK Verse 47 (coming soon)

I don't fuck around. This is what I love to do. But I don't set the dates or do any publishing. I am grateful for the interest, though, and love y'all for reading what I write.

Jadi Borrero, my beautiful friend in Delaware who aspires to be a doctor. I hope we can write something together.

LC and Lay'Anna, love you both.

Danielle Nebres, mom of Charlotte Nebres, author of *Charlotte and the Nutcracker.*

Civahj Naturals (Cosmetic Company for Black & Brown women, men and children), here's to you, too.

FreeCount @ CTHKountUp (told you I wouldn't forget nigga).

Peace out to Brooklyn and the whole NYC.

Big Homie Quest Up Clinton, Dannemora (Andrew Blake hit me).

Ingrid Symone (romance novelist). You read mine, now I read yours. Contact me directly okay?

Danelo Calvacante, who escaped from West Chester Prison in Chester County Pennsylvania. You have 2.4 million people who love you, homie.

Shout-out to the Urban Aint Dead Family.

Last, the saying is that closed mouths don't get fed. Ladies out there reading my novels, I work hard as hell in here to put out my very best material. I'm in Delaware at James T. Vaughn Correctional Center and it would make my day if I could find a "secretary." Maybe you like to write, do research, and are a little computer savvy. You ever think of putting your own book or books out? I may be the man who could assist or even ghostwrite for you. In short, I'm up for some quid pro quo action. It won't hurt to talk on the phone, exchange messages or letters. It would definitely help if you was single. I damn sure am. LOL.

Everyone out there stay up, stay safe and healthy.

Most of all stay prayed up and sucka free.

Contact Lou Garden Price, Sr.

Email: IGHOSTWRITEBOOKS523@gmail.com

P.S. Leave your email and phone number.

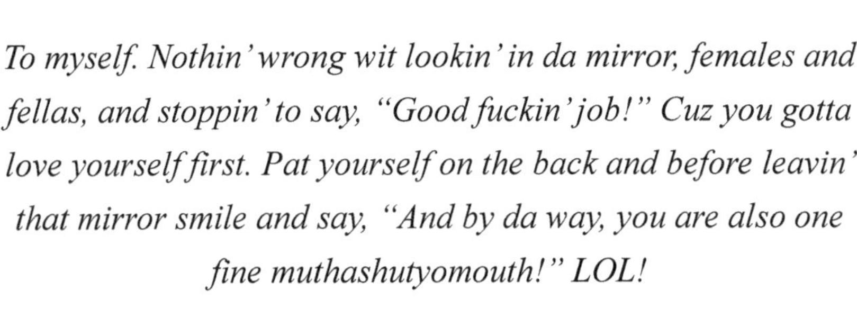

To myself. Nothin' wrong wit lookin' in da mirror, females and fellas, and stoppin' to say, "Good fuckin' job!" Cuz you gotta love yourself first. Pat yourself on the back and before leavin' that mirror smile and say, "And by da way, you are also one fine muthashutyomouth!" LOL!

CHAPTER ONE

Liza Garcia Thomas
The Black Fern Ranch
The Dominican Rep

Nestled in the verdant cliffs of the D.R.'s (Dominican Republic) Monte Cristi, found about 70 miles northeast of the Haitian border town of Fort Liberte and only a few miles away from a massive swath of trees that cascaded down into a valley named El Yaque Del Norte Rio. Way up high on the cliff-top was the so-called La Hacienda De Helecha Negra or The Black Fern Ranch.

It had taken Liza and Sage's real estate agent nearly six months to find the ideal mansion and when Liza had first seen photographs of the Black Fern house, she couldn't believe her eyes. It lacked the cliché Caribbean look and feel, but it fit in with the valley forestry around it. It was extremely high on the cliffs, on firm rock, granite, and limestone. Liza was in love with it.

On her second day there, she couldn't think about the entire beauty and truth behind the trip to D.R. for her and Sage to make a real home there. At first, she'd been a little put off when he had to abort the luxurious helicopter ride over New York City to where their travel agency (The Cabo Frances Macoris) had an amazing large transatlantic jet awaiting them. Liza and Sage had a room on the jet with a Jacuzzi in it! *Unbelievable,* she'd said to herself. *We could've made out, made love, anything. They said oil company and Facebook executives throw parties on these big jets!*

But Liza let that go. She knew her man since they were preteens. There's no way he would have allowed her, Lilly, and Izzy (their baby) - ESPECIALLY his baby, his pride and joy daughter - to leave the country without him next to them *unless* it was totally out of his control. Liza was fine that first day. On the airplane she only had one drink and fell asleep on top of the bed inside of her and Sage's cabin (that's what the stewardesses called it).

Lilly had also fallen asleep in a cabin she'd shared with Daniela Esmé Vallillo aka La Colmillo, which means *"the sting of poisonous snake"* (a moniker earned by her M.O.). Daniela was her alias name because she needed to stay incognito. Since Sage had first laid it all on the line – *including his own neck* – when he came to negotiate and renegotiate Rocky Taylor's previous narcotics deals with her father, The Bullet Proof Don, she had taken a great liking to Sage AKA Coldhearted. Daniela would soon learn that there were many people who called him "CH" for short. Silly how Americans , mostly did that.

People shortened names so that they was easier and quicker to say because of all the syllables in them. Daniela did it but she's Mexicana and in her country, the culture was used to saying a person's full name. Sometimes they'd say the full first, middle, and last *names.* A child carried the last name of the mother then the father in a marriage. In most Latino cultures it was the same way. A family, meaning the woman's family, can bear shame for daughter's having children out of wedlock and having children who only bear one name. That was the name of the mother only. In any event, Daniela went to college at USC, and she was in class with a white girl named Eve and although Eve was only a one-syllable name, people still manage to rip her name apart and only call her "E." It seemed Americans were too fucking lazy to do anything. They thought it would make their days easier to shorten syllables on people's names when all it did was made the person whose name had been shortened have a desire develop of their own: to get the syllable shortener's clown ass out of their face.

Her trued name was Flavia Naomi Santiago. But her and

her father had been talking here and there over the last two years about transforming the multi-billion dollar family empire into something Sage had inherited from Rocky Taylor: *VULKANIKACYD.onion.* Daniela had learned just about everything she needed to know about the Dark Net Site which Sage's SHZ Girlz turned over and taught her. But Daniela also realized that there was much more that she could gain from a long term friendship with Liza and Sage. They loved Daniela and it was sex involved but theirs was a powerful friendship and a closeness above sex.

On Liza's second day in the D.R. Liza was calling her husband with tears in her eyes because he wasn't picking up the phone. They weren't tears of frustration, anger, anxiety, or whatever. They came from deep…down deep in the soul. Elizabeth and Lupé tried to get through to her but they saw her checking five different cellphones, making sure that they were on, she called them with a new burner unit. Sage didn't want anyone - especially enemies or U.S. Feds, who were worse than *any* enemies - being able to pinpoint their exact location by pinging their cellphones. All Liza could think of was the worst –like Sage had trained her to prepare for:

Arrest: If the law had him, they probably had his cellphones and they'd be trying to find her. Cops and feds, most likely the feds, were forever seeking the number one vulnerable person to apply pressure on in order to find out everything they could on their principal suspect. In this scenario, the cops and feds would love to catch Sage slipping and then put

Liza on the hot seat while threatening Isabel with a lifetime of foster care and Lilith Ana Garcia-Thomas with Juvenile Detention as a Ward of New York State. The cops would lie to a woman and a child and the same night eat the tongue, penis, balls, and asshole of a pig for dinner.

Put in a trunk: Sage, as much as Liza tried to picture it, could barely imagine some other street hustlaz kidnapping him but he wasn't invincible. New York City – e.g., *Queens* Borough, *Bronx* Borough, *Staten Island* Borough, *Manhattan* Borough, and the mighty, mighty *Brooklyn* Borough – was loaded with the biggest, baddest, and scariest goons known to man. New York City had a history of birthing some of the most notorious gangsters the streets had ever known: Ellsworth Raymond Johnson (best known as "Bumpy"); Jewish mobster Dutch Schultz, Lucky Luciano, John Gotti, Albert Anastasia ("The Greatest Mobster") AKA Lord High Executioner; Vito Genovese, Carlo Gambino, Lepke Buchatter/Lou Lepke (Murder Inc.), Vincent Mangano, Joe Bonanno, Tommy Gagliano, Joe Profaci, and many others in the Italian and Sicilian Mafia. There was never again a better set-up than *"Murder Inc."* But, getting to the notorious goons - in later years - that had many so-called cocaine and crack dealers shaking in their boots/sneakers, there was Clarence "Minister" Heatley, also known as The Preacher…

The Preacher rolled with his right-hand man John Cuff, who did the real messy work. They were *real* scary gangsters because they stalked New York City in search of the Orcas,

Grizzly Bears, Wolves, and Great White Sharks. They also like buying "debt" like the debt they obtained from former gangster Dave Collins who wrote *"Preacher of The Streets."* Dave had said that R&B crackhead Bobby Brown of New Edition had owed New Jersey drug dealer $25,000.

The Preacher crew got close to Bobby by feeding him crack which he shared with Whitney. In a Bronx luxury co-op, Bobby was beaten, stripped naked, dangled out the window in the nude 30 flights up, and forced to call Whitney. Preacher himself made arrangements with Whitney to bring a half million in cash in exchange for her husband's life.

There were more. Many more gangsters NYC had produced over the years: Gaspar Vetrano, Frank "Black Caesar" Matthews, Kenneth "Supreme" McGriff, Gerald "Prince" Miller of The Supreme Team, Howard "Pappy" Mason, and Lorenzo "Fat Cat" Nichols.

And no one turned on the barbeque pit, using the electric "START" button to fire it up. The Flame burst on under a steel tray and fried the cellphones, destroying them.

"Your man ordered all devices to be cut. Apparently, somethin' happened that has him paranoid."

Liza felt a lot better.

"I can't get over the beauty of this hacienda, this *bedroom*!" Daniela gushed as she opened up all of the curtains with a remote control. "Oh! I didn't mean to do that!"

Liza giggled. "That thing can control the TV, run a hot bath, fire up the Jacuzzi and BBQ pit, locate your phone, lock the doors, flush the toilet if you forgot, spy on everyone in the house, especially your kids…"

"Ew! So you're tellin' me if your mom masturbates—" Daniela started but Liza covered her ears. "Ha, ha, ha, ha, ha, ha, ha!"

They both busted out laughing.

"*Loca, chica,*" Liza said, bumping the Mexican's smaller athletically built hip with her own thick and curvy one.

They stepped outside onto the patio and neither woman had on shoes. They stood on top of glossy black granite with white specks of some sort in it. The chief architect of Black Fern had terminated any plans of creating a patio enclosure for the master bedroom which was on the first floor. When the sun set the occupants of the master bedroom had the benefit of seeing it do so across the Caribbean Sea as it turned crystal clear waters on the shores of Monte Cristi in different shades of orange.

"Go see the lady and the man out there," Daniela reminded Liza who was wearing shorts and a T-shirt. "Somethin' 'bout a yacht or a boat. But…your *clothes.*"

"Oh, shit! I look like walk o'shame!" Liza shrieked. "Help me find somethin' decent to change into!"

CHAPTER TWO

Sage Was Bleeding
The Slaughterhouse
Mt. Vernon, NY

In just about any of the legendary director Antoine Fuqua's movies something really bad happened (not "bad" but "real bad") and the score was to get justice for she, he, or them that was "wronged". Or if something really bad had not already happened then it was about to happen.

Sage was bleeding from the face and down his neck as he put the Sat-phone away. His adrenaline had him sweating and his heart was pumping hard. He took very deep, slow breaths.

Slow the breathing, the heart would also calm down and he'd lose less blood from that bullet that struck him in the face during the shootout. First things first…

He bolted the exit door from the inside so there wouldn't be any unexpected visitors. Only the Rollin 60 Assassins - Kaz, Cumba, and Ammo - had a key to enter their so-called slaughter house. Sage dragged Kaz into the big walk-in freezer, put a meat hook into his mouth, hit the "LIFT" button, and Kaz's lifeless body was hoisted up by his head. The hook perforated a hole in the roof of his mouth and came out through the center of his nose.

Ammo was next. Both dead bodies hung alongside two pig carcasses. Sage idly wondered who had put the pork inside of here. The last man up was Cumba's big mouth ass. He was the primary reason why Sage had laid all three of his top hitters out like Persian rugs. Cumba had raised up on Sage, loud mouthing in a way like he was trying to test Sage's gangster, and he got what he was looking for. His dick in the dirt. And once one of those three killers were smoked Sage felt he had to smoke them all. And now Sage was wondering if he'd have to take out O.G. Bobby Tate and the other Rollin 60's he had close to him.

Y'all niggas hurry back, Sage texted Tate. *Our own top niggas tried to ambush me.*

WTF?!?!? came the reply – from Deuce – who was with Tate at the moment. He was using the TEXTSECURE encryption app that encrypted every message on a mobile phone.

Sage was using the same app, which was cleverly cloaked by TOR, and authorities globally despise it.

IDK 100% but I can guess P plus $$ is answer. No more. Meet later, Sage wrote back deceptively, blaming P-Man. *Stay frosty, stay low.*

As far as Amris and the other girls went, Sage thought about them, but he just hadn't gotten that far yet…

Once Kaz, Cumba, and Ammo were dangling on the meat hooks Sage used two more to hook up Chubb and then had the grinding wench hoist him on up. He put on a pair of surgical rubber gloves and stripped all four corpses. He made sure to search through the pockets. Then he stuffed the clothes and footwear into brown paper bags. He took those to the incinerator, fired it up, dropped the bags into it, and closed the door.

There was an office there with a closet almost filled with clothes. He undressed and put on a black designer jogging suit with new Air Max. Sage had no idea who owned what in the closet, but it was new. There was also a grey and black New York Yankees baseball hat and jacket which he kept to the side.

He used the long orange and black hose with the powerful nozzle attached to wash and rinse the evidence away. First, he prepared the bleach and detergent which was sprayed on every inch of the floor, walls, and ceilings then he let it sit. After a few minutes, he rinsed it all away.

"Man, fuck it," he said out loud and walked into the freezer.

He brought out the electric saws and blades, including a giant chainsaw that could cut a phone pole down in some seconds. He locked himself in the freezer so the loud sounds could not be heard. It took him ninety minutes to chop up the bodies and drop them into the barrels of acid. Following that, he hit the walk-in freezer with the hot water, bleach, detergent, and then the power rinse. When he was done his hands were colder than a polar bear's ass and his jogging suit was ruined.

He made sure the bodies and acid were wheeled out and stored in one of the company's utility vehicles.

"Ayo, papillion, psst!"

Sage had his double Glocks pulled out so fast that it was only a miracle of "hand-to-eye coordination" that saved the two well-dressed Mexicanas. One looked like a straight-up *Papi Chulo* from the *Eastsidaz* with the black and white plaid shirt, dark glasses, khakis with the crease in them, and fur footwear. The other one wore blue jeans, a black leather jacket, and a skully. Neither man had a gun pulled so Sage put his away.

"What da fuck are you sneakin' around for?" Sage snapped angrily.

"Don Armadillo sent who you asked for," the Papi Chulo informed him.

Sage nodded. "Good. You almost got your brains blown all over the sidewalk…You have a car?"

"A dozen cars for two dozen men," Papi Chulo told him. "And you're paying all of our way I was told."

Sage nodded. "Text the Don my thanks. I need a driver. We have a boat two towns over. Take this truck to Greenmore Marina, New Rochelle. It's a four-man job. Bring a car around now."

Sage locked up and got inside of a gold Chevy Blazer. "Papi Chulo" was his driver.

On his way to his boat – with the convoy of Mexicanas and Chicanos following – he sent out a text via *Textsecure* to Liza. He apologized to her and promised her that he'd be on his way ASAP. If he would have left the corpses frozen the entire time he would have met with Tate, Deuce, etc., and *showed* them all four: Kaz, Ammo, Cumba, and Chubb, but Sage had changed his mind. That's why he'd chopped them and dropped them in the acid.

He had contacted the Don (Armadillo) for some hitters to take out all the top crip gangsters he thought he might have to worry about because he had taken out the 60s Assassins. But these Neighborhood Crip cats were dug deep in the trenches out here in New York and they were gonna get that paper.

"Shiid," Sage kind of shrugged and mumbled as Papi Chulo drove them to New Rochelle. *"Imma just lie to Tate and all these other niggas and say Cumba and nem tried to cash in on my death for P-Man by tryna take me out. How they gon' disprove it?"*

They reached the marina and loaded up the 55-gallon barrels onto his and Liza's old fishing boat. It was loaded up within minutes and then they were motoring out of the bay and into the Atlantic.

When they were about three miles out Sage gave the "cutthroat" signal to Papi Chulo who had been operating the boat to stop. Sage dropped anchor and faced his help. "Don't breathe this shit in," he said.

"*¿Que eso?*" one of the other men inquired.

"Shiid, um…" Sage shrugged. "I think they cocktailed it. Muriatic acid, Boric acid, lime, some caustic shit."

They popped the lids, emptied the contents, let the drums fill up with water, and down in the deep they went. Since they were steel drums they had no problem sinking. The body parts were so diced up that the acid almost liquefied them anyway. By the time the boat returned to the marina it was rinsed clean.

A half hour later they were at Garters.

"Just you," Sage said to Papi Chulo. "Papi Chulo is what I call you. What's your name homie?"

"Paul," the *vato loco* said with an impish grin, drawing a low chorus of laughter from his crew.

"Paul?" Sage repeated. "Is Papi Chulo cool?"

"Perfecto," he said.

They entered Garters. It was off the chain tonight. There was a rumor that DJ Paul from *Three 6 Mafia* was coming through to meet with FIVIO Foreign for a meeting regarding some beats FIVIO wanted to buy. It was all over social media. Sage could care less. If he didn't hop on a jet before the sun came up Liza was going to kill him.

As soon as Sage hit his office it dawned on him that Garters was still in need of a General Manager. He left Papi Chulo in the office while he unlocked a door inside the office, reached down on the floor, picked up a lockbox, and locked the door back. He opened up the box, turned it upside down, and said, "For you and your crew," Sage told him as Tate, Deuce, Junior, and several of Garter's dancers entered through the open door.

"Ho, ho, ho! What da fuck?" Sage held his hands up. "Whatta y'all bitches want?"

A slender, badass white girl named Fendi Wendi came up to Sage, nearly naked, and he hugged her. "There's a broken toilet and that new gay bartender needs to be killed!"

Sage shook his head and gently pushed Wendi off of him. "What?! Why? And what gay bartender? The new white guy?"

Wendi nodded. "Nobody that cute should be gay."

Sage hugged and fist-bumped Tate, Deuce, and Junior.

"All of this?" Papi Chulo asked.

"Yeah, spread it evenly with your team," Sage told him. "I'm going on vacation, so I'll be in touch."

Papi Chulo left so Sage looked at the women who had entered the office. "The new white bartender's name is Alan. He has a wife and two kids. Just because he refuses to stare at the girls, make passes, or fuck you doesn't make him a fairy, bitch. It makes him *professional*. I didn't hire him to make you happy any fuckin' way. Now go get my money."

She left with her tail between her legs.

"All you bitches get out there on the floor and make my money!" He dismissed them all.

"*Pimp motherfucker*!" Junior laughed, watching the girls exit. "All that ass under one roof."

Sage shook his head. "Four-fifths of these hoes is havin' male scum bussed in every orifice they got and they takin' on an average of fifteen dicks a shift. Ninety-nine percent of 'em got a dude at home that met 'em here. Y'all know what they tellin' him?"

"I do," Tate said.

"I do, too," Deuce seconded.

"What?" Junior asked them. "What they tellin' 'em?"

"I don't do all what I used to do," Sage mimicked what a stripper would sound like, huge whiny voice and everything. "When I met you my whole world changed. I was lookin' for love the entire time. Now – like Little Orphan Annie – *'the sun'll come out tomorrow'* and – like Olvia Newton-John – *'I'm hopelessly devoted to you'!*"

Laughter all around.

"Damn, y'all niggas crazy," Junior laughed. "What happened to ya face, bossman?"

"I was *shot* in it." Sage stated, cooler than an ice cube.

"Who fuckin' did it?" Tate asked. He'd been quiet because he'd already known that Sage had been attacked because of an earlier text sent to him via *Textsecure* app. Deuce had relayed the message to him because all texts sent through *Textsecure* don't save. Once they were reviewed they disappeared. "Who exactly?"

"Wait outside, J.R.," Deuce ordered the big man.

"No, no, you stay big homie," Sage held up a halting hand. "There's no need, Junior. Take yo family on vacation to Miami, Orlando, or somethin'. Disneyworld. My treat. Just a few days."

"He been training real nice wit the sniper rifles," Tate said. "He's ready."

Sage gave the big man a credit card. "You'll be cool wit that. Fly everybody to a nice vacation spot."

"Thank you," Junior said, giving him a curt nod, handshake-hugging everyone, then leaving.

Sage removed the bandage from the right side of his face and looked into a wooden framed mirror hanging on the wall behind the desk. There was frosty white writing on it that duplicated the Jack Daniel's (bottle) label but it did not obscure his line of sight. Deuce and Tate came up for a closer look.

"Mane, you should go to the hospital. Man, that looks like it's stuck deep in there," Deuce said so close that Sage could feel his breath touch him.

"Look...no hospitals," Sage stated, re-bandaging the swollen wound. The swelling was bad due to the projectile or projectile fragment being lodged so deep through the cheek-bone and soft tissue area under the right eye to the right. But the swelling made it look way worse than it was. "Last thing I need is a doctor callin' the cops, which is exactly what they gonna do. We got enough problems, son. Kaz, Cumba, Ammo, and Chubb are dead."

Tate's head snapped back in surprise.

Deuce was tuck.

"It was them?!" Tate bellowed.

Sage shut the door and locked it, flipping on the *DO NOT DISTURB* sign in red lights overhead.

"I said it huh, Uncle T?" Deuce asked.

Tate was shaking his head. "Niggas closin' in on our first million and…what happened?"

"Chubb was caught feedin' the cops' info – Ammo nem showed me this," Sage stated, displaying to them a printout of outgoing/incoming telephone calls and text message displays which had been intercepted from Chubb's cellphone by Sage's spy system.

"GOD-DAMN," Tate said slowly. "So this dumb nigga know bout da spy devices cuz wasn't he down wit da spy device *crew*?"

Sage nodded. "Guess he figured Choir Boy nem wouldn't be hackin' in on him. Whatever it was, it was dumb. So they had his ass. And just when our helicopters were about to lift off the ground I got an emergency text and jumped off. I get to the slaughter house, see Amris at *G-Bop-A-Lot* store, we wave at each other, go out through the back and down in the basement. Everything - guts, instinct, and luck - was with me and I had my hands on my guns going down that bitch. Soon as the door bolts the shooting starts."

"You think P-Man laid out some game money?" Tate made a statement more than he asked a question.

Sage studied Tate for a moment. "I'm havin' to assume so. How else does anyone benefit from my death? Lilly and Isabel? Liza? They all lose. You and Deuce lose."

"Where they bodies at?"

"*What* bodies? C'mon man," Sage stated. "Why you think I'm still here and not out the country wit my wife and kid?"

Deuce and Tate both understood.

"What about Amris, Blue, Vaynale, and nem?" Tate had to ask. He had a long strained expression on his face exaggerated by the fact that his long hair was only halfway braided. He and Deuce had thick shiny black hair which they maintained by going to hair salons. But for whatever reason both of their heads looked fucked up today.

Sage bandaged then ripped the bulky bandages back off his face. "Fuckin' bullets stingin' da shit outta me…got fuckin' alcohol in my goddamn eye earlier, now I'm getting' a migraine. Fuck!" he yelled out while slamming the top desk drawer. "I trusted them niggas to handle da killin' and they turn for money?! For green fuckin' paper that says PROM-

ISSORY NOTE on it?! I never had no real family 'cept Lilly and Izzy! My father might not have been my father and he tried to kill me the night he killed himself suicide by cop!!"

Tate and Deuce sat dead still.

"That's shits on me, boss homie," Tate finally broke the ensuing silence. "I vouched for dem niggas, thinkin' with better pay, they'd show appreciation, friendship, and loyalty. I'll take the responsibility. I feel mad fucked up right now."

"Me too," Deuce agreed. "I thought we'd be classroom cool but ever since you chose to stand strong wit us around da time I got into dat fight wit da Blood nigga… I was loyal on da strength of friendship. I'm not crossin' nobody for no money."

"It ain't yo fault what dem niggas did, Tee," Sage told Tate. "Fact is it's fuckin' done… and now we gotta worry 'bout Vee, Amris, and that chick clique. Y'all tell me what has to be done."

"They gon' start callin' us in a day or two regardin' dem niggas whereabouts," Tate mentioned. "You head on out to Liza before she pops up."

"Better idea," Sage said as he stood up. "Since we don't have our *Bishop, Knight,* and *Castle* in place to cover Junior in the plan to hit P-Man from a thousand yards out—"

Tate made a face.

Sage faced him at the exit. "Don't tell me y'all spent the last few week's long-range practice shooting for nothing."

Tate shook his head. "Nah, that ain't what Imma tell you.

The spot we found upstate was by the Susquehanna River. A 27-room ranch house, 100-plus acres, a dream spot. J.R. could hit a 1,000-yard target only 60% of 100% - that's a failure in the killin' biz."

"Completely," Joker agreed. "So, where's he 100% at?"

"Seven hundred yards," Tate answered.

Sage nodded. "Twenty-one hundred feet. Damn good distance. That place, where is it?"

"Sidney, New York," Tate informed him. "Junior's a very good learner."

"Let's roll," Sage said.

They went to Sage's house where they came up with a plan on how to deal with the women associated with the Rollin' 60's Assassins.

"You just have no answers at all," Sage suggested. "Tate, you and ya girl Deva just came back from Sidney, New York. Deuce… he been doing what he been doin' – whatever that is."

Sage paused and pulled out a laptop. He used a USB cord and plugged the InvisBox into his burner. A new "Invisbox" Wi-Fi hotspot appeared on the laptop screen. This allowed his burner traffic to be routed over the Tor Network which meant if Amris or any of Kaz, Cumba's, or Ammo's loved ones were to file a missing person's report, the authorities would never trace them at Sage's house. He had their phones.

"Baby, my bad I didn't call," Kaz was telling Amris over a

text. *"Tate wasn't here but we goin' da distance to get da merch correct. I hitchu when we touch O.T. One."*

"So we do nuttin'," Deuce said.

"Sounds good to me," Tate told him. "Long as we ain't gotta chop no four fuckin' bodies up, dice 'em wit da electric band saw, and store 'em for a while in that powerful acid concoction."

Sage showered and called Liza.

"Finally," he sighed.

"Just c'mon!" she whined impatiently.

He kept her on the headset while taking Deuce and Tate down into the basement. "Move that refrigerator," he said to them.

Tate grabbed one end and Deuce the other. Together, they pushed it out of the way. Sage had to punch in the digital computer combination three times before he got it right. It was not a vault-sized safe but it was indeed large.

"Now look," Sage said as he sat down on a cushioned straight-backed chair. "Pull those bags out."

Four canvas material beige book bags were inside the large sage. Inside of each bag were two ladies' shoe boxes, sealed tight with masking tape.

"What's in 'em?" Deuce questioned. "Or… not our business?"

"Nigga," Sage stated sarcastically. "I got you and Uncle O.G. Bobby Tate draggin' them shits out."

"Aight so it's our business." Deuce produced a large

jagged-edge Rambo knife from a sheath fastened to the bottom-center part of his back.

"Want me to show you how to use a machete?" Sage had a huge grin on his face at seeing the Rambo.

"I heard of mufuckin' ax-throwing and knife throwing but you throw machetes, nigga?" Deuce said. "That's some badass shit. If you show me I'll learn it."

"Nigga, you still hold ya fuckin' fork like a baby!" Tate ranked on him. "You ain't learning' shit - especially no ninja shit like machete-throwin'."

"Ha ha," Deuce laughed sarcastically, before continuing with, "…says da Uncle Fester wit half of his hair braided!" Deuce shot back as he cut open one of the boxes… "It's fuckin' cash!"

"Uh huh," Sage said, throwing Deuce a roll of duct tape to seal it back. "What y'all mufuckaz got stashed away?"

"Six K," Deuce revealed.

"About the same," Tate told him. "Wassup, cuz? Why you ask?"

"I promised y'all ya first million and then millions more," Sage reminded them. "Thatta take y'all over a million."

"Aw shit cuz…" Deuce handshake-hugged Sage.

Tate was speechless. "Who we gotta kill? Obama? Trump? Or the Pope?"

Tate embraced Sage.

"Y'all hold it down," was all Sage wanted. "Secure ya shit and let's throw the city in rage and turmoil, starve 'em out."

"What about da homiez? The sellers?" Tate asked.

"They'll survive." Sage had a nice big body Mercedes Benz, the color was known as Tyrian purple. "But if you don't you'll prolly be locked up before I get back. They on us hard."

"Damn." Tate stared at him. "You know how much money we'll be leavin' on the ta-"

"Pause." Sage held a hand up and stared back at him. "Look - goddamn right I know. How you think I just handed you and your nephew a million dollars?"

"Aight. Do what? Go where?" Tate asked.

"Get ya chicks and come to D.R.," Sage stated, hoping that would settle it. He looked at the time on his Rolex Submariner. "Y'all gotta be able to think way bigger than this...if not, we all gonna die in the streets for this bullshit Monopoly Game money. What good is – maan, people are struggling working thirty thousand, forty thousand a year jobs - saving up a couple grand all year – to go on vacation. And we millionaires and *never* leave to go on a beach, see whales or dolphins?"

Tate and Deuce busted out laughing so fucking hard they farted. They promised to be there so Sage exited to catch his flight. Liza had another call so she had hung up on him earlier but once he was on his way to the airport, they hooked back up via Facetime.

"I'm on the highway, Mami," he told her.

"I didn't buy the boat," she told him. "I didn't know what you wanted."

"We'll get one that we can pass on to Izzy," he promised. "Do we need money exchanged or-?"

"This is the D.R., Papi, they take the U.S. dollar or the Dominican peso," she educated him. "Be sure your pilot takes you to Santo Domingo. We're meeting you there and our helicopter is there for maintenance. We're leaving right now on a leased helicopter."

"How long to Santo Domingo?" he asked her.

"Three hours and forty-five minutes," she told him. "Lemme go, *mi amor*. I have to be all cute for you. Hair, fingernails, and toes – all are perfect, and pretty. I know you love my soft and lovely little feet. I got a tattoo on my right foot you'll go nuts for. I can't stop looking at my feet and thinking about my papi."

She had him horny as hell when he boarded the luxury jet. He couldn't wait.

"Yeah, son what up?" Sage asked as he spoke to Deuce and Tate while he was mid-flight to Santo Domingo.

"Bugout not gone," Deuce revealed.

"Huhn?" Sage didn't understand.

Tate spoke up. "Son, we *saw* da nigga and he laughed while driving by."

"So Kaz, Cumba, and Ammo lied?" Sage needed to understand. "They swore!"

"Nigga had a brother who looked like his twin, they call

Flow cuz he rap. He was outside da nigga's crib wit *his* boys in his car," Tate mentioned. "P-Man nem helped perpetrate the 52-fakeout by rapin' Junior's sister, wife, and daughters. No bullets flew and the Black P. Stones got plenty firepower."

Sage shook his head. "So this mufucka still out there. Damn!"

One more headache they had to deal with.

CHAPTER THREE

Mophead, Burn-Burn & B-Kode
"The Oven," Bronx, NY
Early Evening

T ate had several apartments. Not because he was trying to splurge or project the image of a 'hood rich baller' or some sort of P. Diddy, Russell "Rush" Simmons hip-hop mogul or something – although he couldn't help feeling like the "big man." It sure felt good having so much cash, a dozen vehicles at his disposal, a team of killa hitters, Class-A weapons, sniper systems the fuckin' SEALS got, a Latina bitch who was a natural rider and open to do any freaky XXX-rated or erotic-romantical that he placed on the menu.

Like now. She sat silently up the street in a cleverly disguised Department of Public Works truck until Tate came outside with three other men she didn't know. They were carrying a large blue cooler which they loaded into the back of the truck that was marked "Hazardous Materials." Deva had no way of knowing what had occurred moments earlier when Rock and Chubby's mother, Tanya Taylor, had let Tate in almost fifteen minutes earlier.

As soon as she had let him in his other henchmen had rushed in and they'd subdued the frightened woman, knocking her out with chloroform. They taped her hands, stuffed her body inside of her cooler, and used the tape to tightly seal the lid. She would die from the lack of oxygen to the brain.

Next up was Juicy, then Ava, Sonja, Alejandra, Shay, Joyce, Blue Eyez, Diamond Girl, Bhad Barbie, Dojo, Orca, Choir Boy, Wolfman, HK, and Mac-11. Tate had to do it to protect their investment. He pulled together some killaz from South Central and although his nephew Deuce and his boss *"Coldhearted Sage"* had a deep dislike for Damu niggas, Tate broke protocol.

Mophead, Burn-Burn, and B-Kode were a trio of Compton niggas who had did time in the Brig when they were in the U.S. Army. Their charges were all related to drug smuggling and they never made it to Leavenworth or anything. Just 4-, 6-, and 8-month sentences on U.S. Navy vessels. People knew that when a soldier or soldiers were "thrown in the brig" - which is short for *"BRIGANTINE"* - it could be a one-hour stay behind bars or for months at a time while he or she was on board a U.S. Navy or Coast Guard vessel. It can also pertain to any U.S. guardhouse or jail at an installation of the U.S. Army/Military. *One things for certain, them White mufuckaz who designed the slave ships only got better at it with time,* Tate thought to himself one day.

"Baby, I need to know and trust you wit me and wit me fo'real," Tate said to his beautiful Puerto Rican/Dominican woman as they drove the ugly yellow truck to the old aluminum and steel scrap plant right off of Connor and Drummond in the Bronx.

"What da fuck? I am, bro!" she said defensively. "Loyalty's in the Garcia's blood, yo. We not no wack bitches."

"You'll do anything I tell you."

"Not hurt myself or my family," she told him.

"Remember that" he said as they pulled up at the yard.

Deuce was behind them with Noni Honoret-Garcia, her sister. The sun was setting, and it was still warm. There was one man there, the owner. Everyone called him Three Tooth Tommy or Tom. He had three teeth on the top and he seemed content with that because he never got replacements. He was known among the connected to make cars disappear. He crushed them, and melted them down for their various metals, especially the more expensive aluminum. He also stripped them for parts until there was absolutely nothing left except for their body.

In the news more and more lately were thefts for a vehicle's catalytic converter, which was a reaction chamber that typically contained a finely divided catalyst into which exhaust gases from cars' engines were passed together excess air so that carbon monoxide and hydrocarbon pollutants were oxidized to carbon dioxide and water, and nitrogen oxides were reduced to nitrogen and oxygen gases. The "finely divided catalyst" was made up of *platinum, rhodium, palladium,* and *gold.*

Three Tooth Tom salivated over vehicles brought to him and he paid crackheads and dope fiends good money to bring him cars with intact catalytic converters. Any person on earth can understand a man, woman, or child stealing to eat but nowadays, old men and women with babies still secured in car seats were being carjacked in broad daylight, shot in the head, beat to death in Philly as reported by Alex Holley (*Fox 29 News*) and Ukee Washington on *CBS Channel 3* in Philly. But they were reporting that it's an epidemic country-wide.

"*Remember that,*" Deva mumbled, mimicking Tate. "Is that how you gonna talk to me?"

"Fuck…" Tate said, looking at her from outside of the truck. He walked around to her side where she sat with her arms crossed. "I'm sorry. *Los sientos mamita. Se lo juro.* I'll never talk to you like that again. I'm an asshole."

"Plus, you ain't put no ring on it like the Queen herself

taught the singles ladies," Deva reminded him of the Beyonce Knowles-Carter lesson.

"Jay-Z listened, he put a ring on that sweet, sweet thang she got," Noni pointed out. "And she made them babies."

"He was fuckin' her ultra-mega-sunshine stuff from the back and saw the glistening pre-*honeycum* around her lil light brown anal circle…and sweat from his forehead dripped on it and it was over, that's how Blue Ivy came."

"You're a liar and a dum-dum if you think he worked the candyhole," Deva said, jumping out of the truck. "The hop and booty moves Beyonce got. Jay-Z ain't gotta do shit but sit or lay still. We all know it. She takin' it and ridin' that shit."

"Imma put a ring on it." Tate sealed his word with a sweet kiss. "Word on my flag. But you and Noni gotta prove ya'self – *tonight.*"

The talking ceased at that point. Deuce shook hands with Three Tooth and followed him to the scrap yard office, holding a green U.S. Army duffel bag. Tate stayed with the women giving them both semi-automatic Walther PKs [aka "The Lady .380"] because of its their light size and weight. Both charcoal black hand guns were already equipped with professionally-made suppressors.

"Once he crushes the truck…just wait for me to say go," Tate told them.

Three Tooth came out of the office, content with the ten grand he was given for the under the table job. He jumped onto a stack of cars that had already been smashed like soda cans and climbed up into the giant crane. They all watched from below as the huge clamping steel jaws came and picked up the old truck with the ugly yellow color. In a matter of a minute or two, the truck was flattened alone with all of the dead bodies tucked away as safely and as peacefully as they'd ever been. Tate, the Damu Compton cats he knew – Mophead, Burn-Burn, and B-Kode – had wrapped all sixteen of the former Savage Hoodz Boyz and Savage Hoodz Girlz, so that Tanya would never blow the whistle or point the fucking finger the boss's way, she was seat packing, too.

The sounds of the heavy metal creaking, windows breaking, and even the combustion of the tires popping told everyone how powerful the compactor was. Noni and Deva looked at each other.

"You good doin' this?" Noni spoke to her sister in Spanish.

Deva could care less but she was nervous. "Remember that fuckin' Anuel, Becky G, and Daddy Yankee concert and that girl on Bruckner Boulevard?"

Noni got quiet and thought of that hit and run two years back where they hit a seventeen-year old on a bike with Noni driving double the speed limit. She had taken off, and never stopped. Their cousin, Oscar, had fixed the car and painted it. The girl was taken off of life support and died.

Tate was listening to them. "Y'all was never s'posed to talk about it. Shh!"

"We good, yo," Deva told Noni. "If you don't want to I got it. Imma fill 'em up."

"Me too," Noni whispered as the air suddenly had one of the worst aromas ever permeating every inch of air they were breathing.

"Ew!" Noni cried out.

"Oh, my fuckin' goodness!" Deva turned around to try and walk away from it.

Deuce and his uncle never flinched. They knew that scent. And if any member of law enforcement smelled it, they would immediately know that the dead were near. Then, the girls realized what was in the coolers. What all the stealthy behavior was about?

Tate stared at both of them. "Y'all already know...*that it's possible for a person to become a ghost while they're still alive.*"

The truck was taken by the crane to what Three Tooth called "*The oven.*" This was where the truck was melted down and the liquid aluminum would separate and go one way and the steel another. The heat was so high that it completely pulverized the coolers, human remains, bones, teeth, and so forth. Whatever the scrap metal or component in the truck that was not usable, it dried up as black oily dust material.

Three Tooth shut the crane down and jumped on down. "I've been here since 4:00 AM. Time to go get some sleep."

"Niñas," Tate smiled. "Why don't y'all give our friend here a proper goodbye."

Noni and Deva raise their .380s and let loose like target practice on a fence post. ***PHFFFTT!! PHFFFTT!!***

PHFFFTT!! Three shots, four… had the middle-aged scrap plant owner dancing doing the two-step in reverse. Deuce blasted him twice and so did Tate with a shot to Three Tooth Tommy's forehead.

He was done. It was over.

"C'mon son," Tate told his nephew. "Grab his legs, Duke."

They picked him up and it took more work than Tate had anticipated to throw his body into "*The oven.*"

"*Niñas*, back the Escalade out," Tate ordered them. "*En la Calle*. In the street."

While the girls waited, Tate unloaded the guns and threw them into "*the oven*" alone with Three Tooth. Tate and Deuce used large brooms to clear up their tire impressions. With all the dirt Three Tooth did there was no surveillance system around his place. They took the brooms with them, threw them in the trunk, and Deva drove away.

CHAPTER FOUR

It's Only One Bullet
Tres Hermanas Hospital
Monte Cristi, D.R. 11AM

To be allowed into the Dominican Republic all a United States citizen needed was a passport. From the very beginning, Sage felt a welcoming feeling even from the officers who boarded the private plane he had flown in on. Liza was there at the airport waiting for him just like she had said, so there was never a moment where he was lost or waiting.

"Every chick on the fuckin' island is lookin' at my Brooklyn Boy," Liza said as she threw her arms around his neck and they kissed each other like a Pastor somewhere just told them, *"Now, you may kiss the Bride."* Throngs of people passed by them. While they were kissing the dozens of people watching them out their periphery were getting horny because Liza looked so darling and delicious in her Apple Bottom jean short shorts, which her ample backside filled out so nicely. They were white, her asscrack and her phat ass pussy gobbled them up inside the cracks.

They all knew whoever Liza was, she was about to get hammered by some big young black male. Sage showed up fly in a classy gray and black Burberry suit.

"What happened? I missed you," she was hugging him real hard, not wanting to let go. "I don't think we ever apart like that."

"Damn! Turn around, mami," he begged, making her smile all big and dumb-like. "I'm not ignorin' you… I jus'–"

"I know, me too." Liza cut him off in her excitement. She was so happy he was noticing her, because she spent hours readying herself like a virgin in the 1300s did for her King. "I haven't even masturbated but I'm ready to explode already cuz I can feel your hard dick and you smell so good."

"Daniela's here."

"I know but she been goin' out," she told him. "Wit tight security. Her father sent two bodyguards. Farmer Mexican Navy – they got U.S. Navy SEALS skills. They stay in the cottage. Daniela's very respectful."

"Shoulda put your mom and Lupé in the barn," he joked, and she playfully hit him.

They exited the airport, and he directed two airport workers to load his luggage up into the car his wife had leased. "I'm on top of everything, Papi. It's an armored Maybach. Brand new," she pointed at his driver.

"He looks like he's our age – well, mine," her man said, observing the beautiful $500,000 car. It had countershading where the upper part was a darker shade of silver, and the bottom had a lighter tone.

"I'm Julio, I met your lovely wife," he greeted Sage.

Sage shook his hand. "Sage, bro. You speak good English."

"Si, si, yes," the driver replied.

"In D.R., most of the tourist areas are smarter. Speak English, tourists feel more at home," Julio mentioned.

Liza directed Juilo to the Bonaventure Hotel at Santo Domingo. "Why you take so long?" she pressed him while on the way to the hotel. "And your face?"

"Thank you, Julio," Sage said as reached forward and handed the driver a $100 bill. "Radio please?"

"Si, thank you," he said. "Radio, yes."

"Bae, look at yo Daddy's face," he told her.

She peeled the bandage off and a little bit of drool came out the side of her mouth because of staring and thinking.

"Is somethin' in there?" she asked in a tiny voice.

He nodded.

"*Dios mio*," she gasped and held back the tears. "They try to kill you, didn't they?"

He nodded.

She turned to the driver. "To my helicopter…Holà, hello?" she'd called ahead to the pilot.

"To a hospital, Mami," he told her.

She nodded. "Close to our place. Lemme handle it."

They were quiet after that. Julio drove them through the city into the heart of the capital, which was the domain of Christopher Columbus and his descendants. Santo Domingo was home to the huge, imposing Columbus Lighthouse [Faro a Colón]. There's also a monument and museum dedicated to the explorer – a history about a European Spaniard that's inundated with evil filthy White man lies, which was just what Coldhearted Sage said to Liza and their two pilots of the helicopter.

"Them lying thieving no good White slave-runnin' bastards!" he spat without the spit. "Political mufuckaz wit da power use the hardworkin' peoples' money for this rotten, lying, evil bullshit idols, statues, museums, and monuments."

"Señor Columbus discover The New World," one of the pilots, a brown-skinned woman in her 30s, interjected. "That's why we have -." But she was cut off right there.

"Mami, *Señor Columbus* brought Spanish soldiers and mercenaries across the Atlantic Ocean with him on brigantine ships," Sage enlightened her. "Discover, discover, discover – he discovered new places to unload kidnapped Black men, women, and kids from Africa. In the United States, only *fools* believe or say that that fuckin' racist White cracker *discovered...* fuck does that mufucka get the credit? It's a fuckin' historical *lie!* Read the *truth.*"

The helicopter landed on a landing pad outside of a hospital named Tres Hermanas Hospital, where male nurses and female nurses were outside awaiting his arrival. One of the helicopter pilots had called ahead regarding a facial injury of an *"Americano-Moreno"* or Black American. The pilots stayed while Sage was pushed inside in a wheelchair.

One of the nurses wondered what happened to Sage's face. "You his girlfriend, amiga..?"

Liza held up her left hand and showed off the exquisite rock she wore with her diamond inlay, which lit up the entire two rings she wore. The nurse smiled and nodded.

"What happened to him?" the nurse asked.

Liza shrugged. "I was here. *Yo no se.* Ask him."

That was Liza. A gangster's wife through and through. She wasn't volunteering shit. She filled out the necessary paperwork and a supervising nurse came out within fifteen minutes speaking rapid Spanish.

"You know it's a bullet in *tu esposa's* face?" the older, darker, and big matronly supervising nurse fired several fast questions at Liza. She had a very thick Hispanic accent, but her English was clear enough. "Where thees 'appen? Miami? New York? And how can you pay?"

She had her purse. "Credit cards allowed?"

"American Express, Mastercard, and cash," the triage nurse explained that part.

Liza was trying not to get agitated, and they kicked her and Sage out. The Dominican Republic had awesome hospitals, doctors, nurses, and a very decent health system. But the supervising nurse was rubbing Liza the wrong way.

"Can I go be with my husband?" Liza inquired as she looked for her credit cards. She completed the paperwork.

"Pay down one thousand please," the nurse doing the triage showed her a printout.

Liza just reached down into her purse and counted off ten $100 bills of U.S. Currency. Then she walked out of the waiting room with all the men's - and half the women's - eyes glued to Liza's devastatingly lovely, perfect, 100% God-Made booty and beauty. She looked so good that one man thought his wife would miss him staring at Liza's ass and pussy lips – how the crack of her ass was "eating" or *pulling* the shorts up in that motherfucking wiggling thang…and how her pussy print bulged and her slice of paradise was visible like a moose knuckle was in there or something.

"Why don't you close your mouth and go to her on your knees?!" his wife shouted at him.

Liza looked back as the argument broke out. She had a look of exasperation on her face. She was ushered into the room just as a doctor and two lovely Dominican doctor interns assisted him with the minor surgery.

Sage was shirtless because his tie alone was an Italian silk masterpiece by Armani. His shirt, black beater (tank top), and jacket that went with his Burberry suit was $3000. When he dressed he was billionaire fresh. Liza watched him, he looked so nice, and he was so jacked up and ripped from his daily calisthenics, weightlifting, swimming, and other exercises when he had the opportunity. Liza knew these beautiful nurses had eyes for her Black, Brooklyn, New York City Adonis. *Her "Black God." Well, not spelled with the lowercase "g" as permitted by The Book of Psalms 82:6*, she recalled.

"¿Tambien, mi amor?" Liza asked him right at the moment that the 75-year-old Dominican surgeon removed the projectile. He dropped it into a small glass bowl.

"I am now, baby," he stated as the wound was properly flushed and then stitched back together.

"If you have ten thousand U.S. dollars there's the best plastic surgeon in Hispaniola Islands who has an office here," one of the two women said. "All the telenovela stars use him…even baseball guys."

The old doctor was sort of a grumpy cynical person. He added, "You mean Sammy Sosa."

"Who's that?" Sage asked.

"He was around in the 1990s," the doctor washed his hands as he replied. Then he picked up the bowl with the bullet in it.

"Let me have that, Doc," Sage asked but there was a knock at the door.

"I am required to turn over such things to the local police.

I'm sorry." The surgeon opened the door and in came one policeman. "Officer, Mr. Thomas. The shot was days old. Maybe two or three. This is his wife Elizabeth Thomas."

"Liza Garcia-Thomas," Liza said as she rolled her eyes. "C'mon, Papi."

"Excuse me, but I must ask you -" the average-size cop started but Sage was up, allowing his wife to help him get dressed. The doctor left the bullet with the cop and exited. Both of the nurses stood near the sexy Black American trying not to be obvious as they got one more look at his big, chiseled chest, arms, and abs.

"Man, we out," Sage told the policeman. "I just flew in from the U.S. today. I was shot with a stray bullet in the United States and didn't know it."

The cop thought that last part of his statement over. "Didn't know it? Why are you here in D.R.?"

"To live," he told the nosey cop. "We're millionaires. We bought The Black Fern Ranch and everything that came with it. Now, are you gonna play like you some big inspector, and make an enemy outta me? Or are you gonna do the smart thing?"

The officer paused. "Monte Cristi, the beach, the lake, creek, the fruit groves, and that huge house – that's all yours?"

"And my wife," Sage stated arrogantly, ready to leave.

The cop thought about it, absentmindedly rubbing on the chin hairs of his much-outdated goatee. He held the bullet, now in a small clear plastic Ziploc bag.

"Well…it's only one bullet. And *mi abuelo,* my grandfather used to say *some risks are more dangerous these days not to take,* eh?" he recalled the old aphorism and handed the bullet over.

In that instant Sage knew he had met his first dirty cop in D.R. Liza reached into her purse and counted off $1000, which made the cop frown. She kept counting until he smiled at $2200. The cop handed Sage a number to get in contact with him.

"Baby, I had our whole day planned out," she said, her cute lips all pouty. She directed the helicopter to take them to Puerto Plata which sat in the shadow of Mount Isabel de Torres and its statue of Christ the Redeemer. The other thing Puerto Plata was known for was its 19th-century style Victorian timber houses.

In the helicopter, they couldn't keep their hands off of each other. "I'm sorry, baby," he told his sweet lady. She kicked off her Mando Blahniks and put her soft pretty feet into his lap. Her toes were the fucking bomb. She ran into some Korean people in the D.R. and they killed it. He loved her for the new machete tattoo done in red behind her left ear, that said "HEARTLESS" underneath it, which was the name he'd given to his favorite machete.

On her left foot was his name in cursive: *"Sage Michael Thomas, JR."* And she had a pencil sketch made of him; he didn't know where these tattoo artists got such amazing skill, but he'd taken that sketch and put it on the top of her left foot.

He made her mush the bottoms of her toes into his nose and he took real deep sniffs and all he smelled was pretty ass, Liza.

"Damn your feet smell good, baby," he said with a smile that warmed her up inside. The female pilot saw them frolicking around and she was happy for them. "My baby's feet smell like the lotion and soap aisle at *Bath, Bed, & Pretty Beyond Liza.*"

She plucked his ear. "Monte Cristi please!" she said to pilots as she rubbed his ear.

"My whole head hurts cuz I got shot – and you pluckin' my ear, man. You 'bout to get fucked up, bitch."

"You can't hit me, dumbass," she said, kissing him on the ear and sucking it. "That better?"

"Well…*almost*," he lied, pushing that same ear her way.

"You want my mouth somewhere else?" she teased him.

"Damned right," he replied.

"You missed a tattoo, asshole," she told him.

"I got the neck – the machete," he mentioned, and she nodded. "Then my name. My *whole* name."

The helicopter landed and the pilots helped unload Coldhearted's luggage. Liza had already hired a few people to help them. Daniela already occupied the cottage. A half mile up the road was a smaller "guest cabin" that was smaller than the cottage. Liza gave it to her head groundsman and his family. She brought her husband up to speed.

"Sage Michael Thomas, JR.," he finally said aloud. "Wait

a minute. My name is *Sage Michael Thomas*. Where da Sage Michael *Junior?*"

Lilly ran down to meet her brother and hugged him. The pilots took off. Lupé and Elizabeth initiated hugging Sage now.

"Baby, you tellin' me you're pregnant?"

Liza nodded. "I think I have *been* tellin' you, but I wasn't tryna know… plus, I don't get no period when I'm using birth control. But after our daughter, I stayed thicker and…"

"You a *woman*," he almost said emotionally. "A real woman. How long-?"

"Past the first trimester." She had her elbows on the kitchen counter, leaning over to read a bread label.

He was happy and at the same time afraid, but he loved Liza so much. They just hugged. It was all pure affection he had for her and for the first time in their lives together he feared losing her, his daughter, and…

"Your foot."

She nodded as they searched for something to snack on in the kitchen. "What about it?"

"It says Sage Junior. Sage Michael Thomas, Junior." He found a hairy mango on the top shelf in the refrigerator and Liza stopped him.

"We have a cook and housekeepers," she reminded him, leading him out of the kitchen into their dining room. "Just sit and they'll bring food. This way, we have 'us' time. Mommie,

Papi's hungry…About the tatt. I told you when we were in Cali and then that night after the swimming pool freak-off."

"When Naiba was kicked out?" he asked.

She nodded. "But I wasn't trippin'. I knew. That's why I started takin' my supplements. Well…"

"You make smoothies and pop vitamins just like me, so I saw nuttin' different," he said.

"You were too busy staring at all this killa curviness God gave me," she smiled.

"Gave *us* goddamnit," he told her. "You still never told me."

"Didn't wanna jinx it 'til after the first trimester. Papi, with everything goin' on in the city, I don't wanna go back or be under any stress. And just so you know when I did go for my check-up and they saw the size of the fetus, my doctor was livid that I ain't go in sooner. But she was able to say that the baby is healthy, she's glad I put on weight, and it's a boy. That's where the *insight* on the *Junior* tatt comes from." She was happy as a lark to be saying it. That she was giving her husband a boy and his name was already decided. "You okay with that?"

"A son? Hell yeah. You findin' out without me? *I.D.C.,*" he told her. "A little me times two. Damn."

Lupé brought in Isabel who lit up like lights at the sight of her daddy. Elicia Sales came in with a black "baby bag" strapped over her left shoulder. The chubby, older black woman was known for her wigs only because of how bad they looked on her. She had become a family friend and Izzy had taken to her from the start, Sage believed, because of all of Ms. Elicia's fat. Babies loved big women because they were so soft and warm to feel on and sleep against.

"Boy, you need to jus' hush," Ms. Elicia had joked with Sage once as he'd told Tate and Deuce about the big black woman whom Liza had hired to start early home school for Izzy. Elicia was a people person. They all liked the retired Montessori/Private school English and math teacher.

That day, nearly five months back when Sage had introduced Ms. Sales to Tate and Deuce, Sage had made a remark about Elicia not teaching Isabel what he called *"white man lies."* She had stood firmly and explained to Sage…

"…need to jus' hush," she'd stated. "Your wife told me that you were skeptical about my *agenda*. I teach by the laws of New York State Board of Education requirements. I'll have you know that I do not teach *lies,* I teach the *language*…to little black boys and girls. I come highly qualified. A lot of Black families call on me. I'll have your lil' one ready if you'll accept me."

After she had laid that on him they were cooler than cucumbers. Elicia became more and more like the "Mama" in the house when she came. Sometimes, she left early to beat the traffic, but she lived in Queens, by herself. Her husband had died, and her four children were married so they had their own houses. When she asked Liza if it would make sense for her to move near Mt. Vernon or to Mt. Vernon, Liza answered in the affirmative. She sold her Queens' residence and rented an apartment in a rather ritzy enclave of Mt. Vernon – just minutes away.

Now, or when, *the D.R.* popped up on the itinerary, before Elicia could say anything about the trip, Liza was on the phone *begging* Elicia to jump on a commercial jet to Monte Cristi. She readily agreed. She was actually feeling heart-pounding anxiety the moment she'd first learned that the couple was going to be purchasing a second home in the Dominican Republic because she would feel such a total loss if she couldn't see Isabel. They had grown so close. They all had. And, Elicia didn't mind going outside of her job description whenever Liza or Sage demanded it.

Sage, Liza, Lupé, Elizabeth, Lilly, Isabel, and Elicia all sat down to have lunch. Liza had hired a very capable and experienced housekeeping staff, including a cook, and they handled almost *everything*. All of them were Dominican women. Most of them were the wives and daughters of the groundskeepers outside.

"How many of 'em is it all together?" Sage was asking when he saw a very young Dominican girl pushing a cart into the dining room.

"Eleven? Fourteen? Nine?" Liza answered him. "Papi, they have younger ones who pitch in after school… there's like a couple sisters, some cousins, aunts our age – the men are outside as groundskeepers, landscapers, and…"

Before she could finish, Daniela Esmé Vallillo came in, the

daughter of Sage's dope/cocaine connect. She had become super tight with everyone.

"No bodyguards?" Liza teased the beautiful Mexicana from the North.

"Smells great…where's the food?"

The maids brought out two enormous round platters that contained the most delicious looking dishes of *Blackened Salmon Pasta Alfredo, Air Fryer Garlic Asparagus,* and a crispy *Crossover Tropical Salad* that contained lettuce and various sliced fruit. Everybody ate more than they talked because the food was so tasty. For dessert they were served bananas foster. The conversation picked back up but not with Sage and Liza at the table. They had retired to their master bedroom suite.

"Your face hurt?" she asked her husband sweetly as she pulled open the glass doors and panoramic windows and sat down on one of the huge, overstuffed recliner chairs.

He stood looking out at the vast Caribbean Sea and all he could spot out there were a few boats and sea birds such as seagulls, skimmers, and petrels out on patrol. He looked around, shook his head to answer her, and slowly undressed.

"I been takin' Percocets," he told her, watching her stand up to close the doors and curtains.

"Leave it, Bonita Chica."

She smiled impishly. "Every boat out there…they have binoculars and telescopes."

"Mhm." He used her cellphone real quick to order a

powerful telescope to look at the space with as well as one to look out over the sea.

By that time she was going into the bathroom. They ended up showering together. And later, they were back in the bedroom on the polar bear rug rubbing lotion on one another. The sun was setting, and they were watching every moment of it. Liza began to cry.

"What? What is it, Mami?"

"They tried to kill you, man." She said and sniffled. "I saw da fuckin' bullet! It coulda came out da back of your head or somethin'."

"Aw shit," he murmured. He felt bad but also guilty. He thought he should be straight with her. "I know Liza, I fuckin' know. Truth is that insurance and inheritance money was a blessin' and a curse. Nobody gets to go scot-free in da game. Dat fuckin' Mt. Vernon, the B-X, the strip club, our house and cars… I'm a young fifty-thousand-watt livewire and niggas are jealous. Them old ass niggas especially."

"Lemme start a fire," she said while reaching over to the bedside table. All she had on were her silk thong panties so when she rolled over and up onto her knees, he instantly became hard.

"You gonna have to show me all the tricks you had put on the house or installed into it," he said when she grabbed two remote control devices. He let her show him how to start the fire inside of the fireplace located in the master bedroom suite.

"Okay." She started the fire. The sea air came in along with that salt scent from the sea.

He wrapped her up in his big arms and made her feel so protected and secure. "You another reason haters wanna see me dead. Don't feel bad for it. I'm just being factual. Word on everything."

She understood it. "Females despise me because of you. Members in my own family I know are envious. So I get it. I was just reading how this Indian-Canadian college girl, 19 years old, was an actress on the *CW* television channel and starred in *Diary of a Wimpy Kid.* She cut her jealous, cowardly, ex-boyfriend off and he savagely murdered her. This pussy from British Colombia named Gurjinder 'Gary' Dhaliwal."

"You mean we seen it not read about it," he reminded her.

"I said *read*? I meant *watched* it on Oxygen Channel's *Killer Relationship with Faith Jenkins*," she said, correcting her error. "Shot her, killed her, then after death, he took a big ass hunting knife to her. I say it cuz we talkin' 'bout hatred jealously. That punk-ass coward was jealous of shorty. Look at her."

"I am." He had turned the giant 86-inch television on. "Goddamn this a big TV, ma. Look at her. Who's them two?"

He was pointing at two women who had been interviewed on the show.

"Rosaleen Batalia, Maple Batalia's sister," she told him,

yawning. "Karen Kang and Natalie Sheek were Maple's friends. They all were beautiful."

"I agree, they look gorgeous," he mentioned, turning the TV off. "Now, you… no more sad stories. Cuz the baby needs to hear happy sounds. And Daddy making love to Mommy…"

"Mmmm," she wrapped her arms around his shoulders, giving him a deep wet tongue kiss.

He reached down and pulled off her white lacy silk thong and smelled it. "Mm-mmm!"

For the next several hours they made love with only the moon and stars outside as a witness.

CHAPTER FIVE

The Liza Rosa
Liza's New Yacht
Caribbean Sea, D.R. – Noon

"So lemme get this straight, Papi," Liza was saying to Sage right after she helped her down from the back of the new Silverado extended cab pickup truck. "Are you sayin' we're broke?"

He only wore shorts, he was bare-chested and barefooted, but they were at the beach at the bottom of the hills and cliffs of Black Fern Ranch. Liza, Daniela, Elizabeth, Lupé, and Lilly all wore various kinds of bathing suits or bikinis. Their yacht had been purchased and delivered to the Black Fern Marina which was where they were headed to.

"No, no one's broke," he stated. "I had Melissa remove my name off of Lilly's trust so once she turns eighteen, she'll have immediate access to three million dollars. Plus with investments...it could be double that. My trust has now been invested to $5 million and hidden."

"Hidden for what? The cops?" she asked.

"For every reason you can think of...including – as you say – cops," he said with a shrug for emphasis. "I spent more than I wanted on this place."

Liza kind of paused. "Hold up. You sent me here to find us a place to live and I used *Pinterest* to give you a virtual look at everything. I bought what I thought you'd like because we're both security fanatics. No one can scale the crags and rocky cliffs behind our house and from the front, we could see out for two miles down the mountain."

"I'm not knockin' none of that," he assured her, seeing that she was becoming upset. "I only made one comment about it bein' a price tag we should've negotiated through Melissa. You paid out $25 million."

Liza was mad now. "Don't forget I emptied the Bargains Galore account."

He just abandoned the conversation. "C'mon, mama. It's all of us chillin'... is that a shark?"

They were all on the 57-foot "*Black Fern Ranch Wharf*" as the sign indicated. Daniela pointed at each end of the white sandy beach to show Sage what part of the beach was owned by the ranch.

"That's all our property, 'bout two hundred yards of beach?" he asked.

"Yep," Daniela replied.

To access the beach they had to drive a mile to the left on the main service road at the bottom of the hill. They had to go through two locked gates to get to the beach and to their wharf.

"My goodness, that is a beautiful boat," Lupé emphasized as they began to board Liza and Sage's new yacht. As they all got on board Liza received a phone call from New York that kept her distracted from the group. Sage took notice but didn't intervene.

"Hijo," Elizabeth approached Sage. "Youse spent millions. You won't draw the law your way? Because I'm a -"

He cut her off. "*¿Paranoico?* Mama, tranquilo. Es Tambien. *Todos es Tambien,* I swear to God."

The yacht they'd purchased was actually "financed property" of theirs that they had ordered through the Italian luxury boat builders "RIVA." The price tag was 16 million USD. The *122 Mythos* was the largest aluminum "planning" (e.g., planning meaning: *to rise partly out of the water as a hydroplane does at high speeds*) yacht that the RIVA manufacturers had ever produced. It was sure one hell of a gift to his wife. Liza did not expect what he did next… Once everyone was onboard the vessel only Sage and Liza needed to cross the short plank but she was talking in motor-mouth Spanish back and forth on her cellphone.

"You good?" Sage asked her.

She tried to walk past him.

"Hey…hey, hey!" Sage grabbed her arm. "You on the phone talkin' biz when we s'posed to be chillin'."

"I'm chillin' man, lemme go," she yanked her arm away.

"Kiss me."

She smiled half-assed but kissed him.

"C'mon, Sage!" Elizabeth shouted at him, wondering what they were doing.

"Okay!" He held a hand up and pointed at the right side of the yacht. Liza looked, a little puzzled at Sage's behavior, like why let everyone else on while keeping himself and Liza at the ramp/plank. "Now!" Sage yelled over to Liza's mother.

"You fuckin' asshole!" Liza squealed and busted out laughing. She was beyond thrilled to see the name of the boat: *THE LIZA ROSA.* She was such a crybaby as she looked up at her mom, her aunt, and then at Sage.

"You still mad at me?" he asked as he dried her tears.

She shook her head. "No," she sobbed at such a huge gesture. "I'll never forget all the times you made me feel like this."

"You my best friend, my wife, and my baby mama," he joked.

He dropped to one knee, and she laughed. "Boy, watchu doin'?"

He took a deep breath. "Doin' it right. Liza, I wish for nothin' more in this world for you to be my wife AGAIN?"

She nodded, as happy as ever. He stood up and they kissed. They embraced as firmly as any two people could and kissed some more. Liza's lips were naturally a deep pink but today, they were shiny in the 88 a wrap-around sarong that he could see through. Daniela's security detail were solid men, very respectful, and Sage noted that because although they were well-paid, it had to "hurt" them to see top-notch bitches with beautiful bodies, near naked asses, phat pussies (their imprint and pussy hair visible), and Sage making them howl like horny lustful she-wolves.

One of the bodyguards knew how to pilot the yacht because Don Armadillo had one similar. As they pushed off and set out to sea Sage spoke with the alert killer. "They call you Sonny," Sage mentioned to him.

He nodded. "Correct, sir," Sonny spoke pretty good English.

"I spoke to Daniela," Sage revealed to him. "About y'all."

"Okay," Sonny said.

"Yeah," Sage went ahead and explained the entire content of their conversation. "We're plannin' on stayin' here at least a month. Dani has to leave for her underground sex club memberships here and there. If you and your men want women we can supply them. Or..."

Sonny glanced at Sage. "Or?"

"If you have your own girls, wives -"

Daniela heard the conversation as she approached them at the primary helm station. "Cold, uhn-uhn. I agreed to overnight hook-ups, pool parties, or whatever but only overnight with strippers, and happy-ending types of internet chicas but *no repeats* with girls like that. This is the D.R. There's a lot of hungry wolves out there so we don't want *repeat* whores bein' used by robbers to case Black Fern. Females are a dime a dozen, right Sonny?"

"Not ones like you or Miss Elizabeth," Sonny mentioned.

Sage grinned. "You like Elizabeth, Sonny?"

Sonny got nervous. "I never mean to -"

"None of my men have wives," Daniela revealed to Sage. "Never, ever, ever, ever, repeats on Black Fern. Huhn?"

"*Nunca, Patrona*, (never, boss lady)," Sonny said.

"These are my family," Daniela stated, winking at Sage. "Protect them like you protect me and my father. Whenever any of you are off – fun time. Don't volunteer any information to those slimy club rats. I don't care how cute the smile or how perfect the booty is, what dance they can do, what car they drive – I'll bet anything they owe more on the car than they do their house. Never trust them grimy bitches. They have cobra fangs and for some extra cash, they'll sell their own babies and lie on the baby daddy. Fuck bitches."

"Damn!" Sage took Daniela with him. "Let's see more of the boat."

The 122 Mythos was designed with a focus on fuel consumption and cruising range. Therefore, it featured an active stabilization system to improve trim, and while – at more than 37 meters long and 7.6 meters in the beam – it was no speed machine; with a pair of MTU-12-V-4000-M-93L engines, an owner could expect 27 of the most refined knots it was possible to experience. The Mythos can be specified with three, four, or five cabins, in all cases, buyers were gifted with a twin tender garage, an assortment of panoramic views, a Jacuzzi, a second helm station, and the happy knowledge that the buyer's boat was better than the one next door. "*The Liza Rosa*" was superior and it had five cabins.

Daniela and Sage made their way down to the master cabin after making sure that Lilly and Izzy had on sunscreen. Lilly had said, "I'm black, mostly, so I don't need it, but Izzy looks like my cousin Liza's skin. She needs it more."

"That's crazy, Lilly," Dani told her. "You and Izzy both are maybe a shade darker than Liza and she looks white. Black or not, the sun can cause cancer in your skin and you can die. The sun don't care who it kills so respect it."

Lilly sucked her teeth and sprayed the sunscreen on. Sage kissed Liza as he and Daniela entered the lovely room. The bed was large and so was the ceiling at 6 feet. There was a small floor-to-ceiling closet to the left of the head of the bed and another on the right. Liza was again on the cellphone. This time she had her ear buds in and was speaking with several of the girls that Tanya had brought on to help assist with Bargains Galore. Sage and Daniela both laid back on the bed to check it out.

While Daniela was turning on the 48-inch wall-screen TV, Sage got up on the stripper pole and tried to amuse the girls with a stiff dance. "Is that the fuckin' *robot* dance you doin', son?" Daniela clowned him in her best Brooklyn/New York City accent.

Liza took her earbuds out, catching Sage's attention.

"¿Que fue? Hablame, Mami," he said, urging Liza to tell him what was bothering her.

"I spoke to our security people earlier cuz I seen someone walking around the perimeter of our Mt. Vernon property," Liza told them.

Sage stopped screwing around. "Show me," he said. These days, a person could be 12,000 miles away from home and still be able to monitor every inch of it. The "DOORBELL CAMERA" technology told even the most ignorant of laymen that.

Liza gave Sage her iPhone business cellphone, and they hooked it up to the 27-inch Dell computer that was inside of the master suite of *"The Liza Rosa."* Liza did some quick typing and Sage read the security reports. Their security company kept watch over their assets in their absence, which included Garters, Savage Hoodz Records, their Mt. Vernon home, the BG Warehouse (Bargains Galore Warehouse), the BG stores, etcetera. If anyone came into range of their cameras and in some cases their "audio-visual" capturing cameras, they could access those recorded files.

"Cerca de alli..." Liza was whispering as she "thumbed" through the digital files.

Daniela saw that Liza was speeding and that something was worrying her. "Mami, *aflojar la paso,* (slow down). There's no rush. Just say who it was."

"The feds or cops the security company said," Liza let them know. "But that ain't it. None of my SHZ Girlz has been around. And nobody can find Tanya or Chubb."

"Hm." The first thing Sage thought about was Tate and his group. *Because I ain't tell dat nigga to hit Tanya but it ain't no tellin'...He's Security Boss, though, but damn son.*

"Mirar, ellá!" (Look, that's her). Liza pointed. "I've seen her before, but one other woman and a skinny guy were there with her on the eleventh."

Sage glanced at a nearby calendar and said, "Two days ago," as he watched Daniela toy with the master suites music. An expensive Bose stereo system which mounted into the wall next to the television.

Daniela started off with Karl G's bangers first because Karol G was the baddest Latina she'd ever seen or heard: *"Leyendas"* played first as Sage spoke in hushed tones with Liza. Sage made a *RedPhone* call and found out that Tate and his crew were in Santo Domingo with Deuce, Deva, Noni, and some others that Tate and Deuce brought along. Sage decided not to tell his wife that her two favorite cousins were in the Dominican Republic.

"Ooohh!!" Daniela squealed when she heard Karol G's hit

single *"Provenza."* Daniela started singing the lyrics to every song that came on of Karol G's: *Tusa.*

Then, the brand new *"Manaña Sera Bonito (Bichota Season)."*

"That's that Westchester County Municipal Drug Task Force Lieutenant Claudia Blackstone," Sage informed his wife as she continued thumbing through all of the digital security logs. "That's some fly technology. It's high color quality, high definition."

Daniela unleashed the round silver sarong ring and pink silk belt sash holding the beautiful Prada sarong up. When she did, Liza and Sage glanced back at the sensuous swing and sway of her young hips. The music started playing J Balvin's hit song *"Mi Gente"* and Daniela turned it up.

"Wet pretty pussy music right there, huhn, Mami?" she asked Liza who still had her mind on New York. But Liza emitted a small smile, nodding her head. "That Claudia…she *wants* Coldhearted Sage Michael Thomas. I *know* it."

That got Liza's attention. "She's a very powerful cop who has the Mayor's ear and can affect our liquor license if the MPD wants to play dirty." She looked in his direction, but it was hard to take her eyes off the Mexican hot girl.

"She's right. But go after her?" Tate had to hear it from his wife. "You saying I should seduce her?"

Liza nodded as Daniela opened the cabin door, peeked out, shut it, locked it, and scooted back onto the bed where she finished getting naked. Sage was so horny now that he could barely hide his enrage bone. He went over to Liza and pulled her with him to the bed, shedding what little they both wore.

"Fuck your pregnant wife," Daniela whispered as the hot bombshell fingered her goosy honey hole with one hand while the other fist rubbed gently against his back, buttocks, and then she grabbed ahold of his scrotum from behind. She licked his neck and right ear, continuing to talk sensually and nasty to him.

Liza's luxurious long black hair was between curly and wavy, but it still fell all the way down to the center of her booty cheeks. Her hairstylist had to clear the entire day whenever she had Lilith come in for washing and setting. Liza's hair was very thick and healthy. And if she wanted braiding, fuhgeddaboudit, the entire day and some of the night. She put it in a quick ponytail and then turned to French kiss Sage.

"I love you so much," she told him. "You're... my... man... my... husband... My... God... I... worship... you... Only... you." Following each word was a sweet kiss as she went downward.

"Goodness, y'all are so sweet," Daniela stated with a lump in her throat. "Never had I seen true love. Thank you for sharing everything with me."

"We love you, Dani," Sage said.

Liza clutched Daniela's hand as she clutched her husband's giant manhood in her small right hand. She rolled her face and nose against the heat emanating from his great cock and balls. She immensely adored the musky scent of him and the feel of his "dick skin" on her.

"Mm, *my* dick," Liza reaffirmed. If she could hug that big shit she would. She took him in her sweet mouth and spun her pink tongue around and around the fat plum-sized head as his clear pre-cum slowly squirted forth. The slurping and the wild sounds she made deep in her throat only served to make them both hotter.

"Damn, Liza! You need daddy's dick, huhn?"

"Uhn! I need it," she repeated and without her cunt being touched she felt it spasm. "Oh my God, Sage, I fuckin' had a mini and wasn't bein' touched!"

She got into the 69 position with him and almost immediately her mini orgasm juices started pouring down the sides of his face. But his cock went **BOOIING!** It inflated, grew longer, and his big balls drew upward, indicating that he was on the cusp of great pleasure himself. However, the women who knew Sage also knew that he could let off a massive stream of semen and not go soft. Once he caught the scent of his beautiful Puerto Rican and Dominicana's copious mini orgasm cream he pulled her glorious alabaster buttocks apart and in towards his face, plunging his nose and tongue into.

Daniela watched them closely. All the while the red-headed Mexican Irish girl gently and lightly pinched her pea-sized clitoris. It smelled like every man and woman's fantasy inside the cabin - like real good pussy. And it looked like a scene from those throwback *www.tapemaninc.com* DVDs with "JOE PRO" or one of those sex stories published inside of *"Wet Dreams On Lockdown"* by *UrbanAintDead.com.* The way Daniela was masturbating was so hot. She was on her clitoris one particular way, and she looked very sexy as her golden skin slowly became awash in a steamy sheen of sweat. It was very easy to start sweating in the Dominican Republic during the Summer months.

"Damn, Liza, shit that feels good! You gon' make a nigga fuckin' buss!" he cussed and humped up and down, up and down, up, down, up down. She was one arm at a time while her head bobbed up and down. She had one hand on the bed using it like a kickstand or something. The other was being used to titillate and gently massage her husband's balls, which she liked to lick and suck. "Liza, Mami…ohhh, shit she got me seein' double, Dani!"

Liza wasn't fucking around. She stroked him with her hands while talking to him. "I'm 'bout to get up, Daddy."

"What? N-no!" He wrapped his arms around her waist, touching her bald cunt. "I need this shit right now."

She heard him smelling her honey holes and crevices. "I'm not goin' nowhere but Mami needs to eat. Lick it and smell it one more time."

He did exactly that. She loved that shit.

She repositioned herself back in front of him and buried him inside of her throat. This time she had both hands to work with, and one of them she used to gently clamp onto his big nuts and jacked them off in rhythm with her miraculously swallowing his sweet chocolatey dick.

"Mmm, shhk, gllrrrb, ahhhuunnn," she made her usual wild sexy cock-sucking noises. "Smack, smack, gllrrrbb, gllrrrbb, ahuunnn, shhk, *ohmyfuckinggodIlovethisinhumandick!*" She said it with no breath, no breathing, no pause, no syllables. Only a hot spirit and sweat.

She twisted her hands as she bobbed down and just when he was about to buss off the sticky nut, she stopped cold.

"FUCK!" he shouted. Elizabeth came to the door and knocked.

"We see whales! And dolphins!" Elizabeth said.

Liza sent her mother away. "We'll be up in a while!"

Elizabeth left.

"Why you stop? I thought you wanted the nut?"

"I did. I do. I'll lick the *pee* off your dick." Liza wasn't laughing. "Claudia Blackstone, you'll have to seduce and fuck but she's not old, not ugly. Don't you *ever* bring no baby into this world that don't belong to *Liza Thomas tu Tambien?*" she warned him.

"Swear," he stated to her, pulling her to him where they kissed.

Liza was in tears that were almost as wet as her tight mango which she was slowly impaling on this super-hard dick.

"Mami," Sage paused but Liza was in a fucking mood.

"I told you, baby. I just love you so much and we gon' have a son together. A *man!* Another... ooooooooouuuuuuuu...

yyyeeeeeeaaaaaahhhhhh, you are touching and feeling your son where you buried the seed for him right there. Stay still, Daddy," she stroked the back of Sage's neck and kept speaking while making love slowly. She humped faster, talking dirty as he sucked her beautiful nipples. "Sage!"

She rocked back and forth then swiveled her hips in 360 degrees circles. It wasn't long before she turned it up and stared down at the adorable Mexicana who was having fun watching and masturbating.

"You want your ass fucked while he's fuckin' you?" Dani asked her.

"Fuck my ass!" Liza nodded.

Dani used the natural lubrication from Liza's juicy cunt to penetrate her with her index and middle fingers. At first, Liza's sphincter muscles wouldn't budge but when Sage sucked on his baby's gorgeous titties it opened her ass up.

"You really want a dick in there, dontchu?" he whispered to her, licking her sweaty neck and ear. "I seen you checkin' out some of these Dominican men in the airport."

"Yeah but I just want my daddy inside me," Liza whimpered.

"I'll let you get fucked by some new dick and I'll be there to watch ya back, okay? I know damn well you want a new dick to taste and buss in your mouth, your pussy, and inside your phat beautiful asshole. Just say yeah and I promise you some wild group sex, baby, so you can take your pick."

Dani's fingers were inside of her, wiggling and banging, as

Liza thrust her pussy and ass back and forth, crying and screaming, and getting ready to cum on Sage's dick and Dani's fingers.

"Yeah, Daddy, I wanna be fucked. I'll do it! I'll suck his dick real good, too… and I'll let him bone my pretty asshole but no pussy while we're pregnant, Daddy," she whined and let out one of the wildest wails he'd ever heard her make. He watched her shake and wail as she pictured it, she was staring away from Sage, thinking about a man she'd seen in the airport. A brown-skinned Dominican man who'd stared at her cleavage and the camel toe imprint of her chubby cunt lips. She remembered that the man was a little older, bald, had a mustache, and was big all around.

Liza was picturing that man having at least a six-inch cock that was as thick as her wrist, and she dreamt of it spewing at least an ounce or two of cum at a time. Seeing her gasp and cum all over his dick like she was doing made him grab hold of her wet and slippery buttocks and squeeze on them hard.

"Fuck, Liza! Oh Fuck! Oh Fuck! Yeah!"

"Oh my god! Oh my god! Oh my god! Oh my god! Oh my god!" Liza was screaming, *"Save me god"* as she came down from the multiple orgasms she experienced.

Liza disconnected and fell over onto her back. Daniela got on top of her and some brand-new humping began. The two bombshell women fucked each other. Sage watched as another round began. The way Daniela was pushing her ass up and down, causing her clit to kiss his wife's, made his mouth water when he stared at her wet pussy.

He just went ahead and stuck in his face in her ass. Daniela yelped. He spread open those buns and bore a hole into hers. She went buck wild and reached the climax she'd been looking for over the past hour and some change. Once they were done they put their scanty clothing back on and had some laughs as they went back out into the yacht's sun room where the bar was.

"Look at Izzy, knocked out," Liza said to Sage.

On the sofa with a jacket over her was two-year old Isabel asleep on her back with her arms wide open just like her mouth. Elizabeth and Lupé were making sure that the baby was okay as they sat having drinks and a good time.

"Head back in!" Sage called up to the helm.

"Okay!" Sonny called back.

When they reached the Black Fern Ranch Wharf Sage, Liza, and Daniela dived into the water to rinse off the scent of sex. Afterward, the boat was anchored and secured they called for a ride to get back to the ranch.

CHAPTER SIX

The Arrival of Amris
Black Fern Ranch
D.R. – Early Evening

The Black Fern Ranch was not easy to access even if authorities wanted to reach the main residence. At the bottom of the hills, where the main access road was, one could do all the driving that they desired from that point. Four-wheeler ATV's – like the Odyssey – could manage which was why Liza leased six of them with an option to buy them later.

It was well-known, however, that there were no paved roads in Monte Cristi at all. The government liked it that way because it gave the countryside and the D.R.'s waterfront properties a persevered virgin look for potential tourists to see from the air whether online, in travel magazines, or any publication that promoted the Dominican Republic worldwide. Big money came to the government and many of its people. There were about 9,366.000 inhabitants in the country, 75% of them were of mixed race. The government loved its money.

Liza loved the beach. She was half Puerto Rican, half Dominican. When Sage had spoken of "vacationing" for a while and letting her choose the destination to make up for his past transgressions, neglect, and so forth, she'd already had the Dominican Republic in mind. She had family there that Elizabeth, Lupé, Maria, and so many others in the Garcia Family had visited when she was much, much younger. Liza's relatives were fishermen, and cooks, and some of the women were teachers and midwives like her mother and Aunt Lupé were today. Her father was *"Bienvenidos"* Carlos Juan Jaramillo-Garcia, a Puerto Rican- her *"supposed to be"* father - which had always caused a rift between Liza and her mother because when Elizabeth was younger she was running around with too many boyfriends to count. It was also very complicated to talk about with anyone except Sage.

For the most part, Liza's family had worked hard all of their lives to get out of the slums of Santo Domingo by working close to the beach. They were all sun-bearing *"beach people."* They referred to themselves as *"La Gente de Playa,"* or simply as islanders, which in their language was *isleños.*

"This nigga that's s'posed to be my dad -" Liza was explaining to Sage as they soaked in the large hot tub.

"I'm Daddy. I love you. I protect you. Provide for you," Sage reminded her. She sat between his legs, his long powerful arms around her from behind, his right hand holding her big, round, left breast, his left holding her right breast. The water was soapy, scented with jasmine, myrrh, and sweet cicely. Half of the water was coconut milk. "Fuck that mufuckin' bastard. I sacrifice my life for my Liza. My sweet Liza."

She turned to kiss him. "Sorry, you're right. One hundred percent right. You're the only man to ever be a real *man* for me and you deserve that Daddy title. Not like one of these hood rat ratchet hoes who done fucked every nigga in America and wanna call some used-car-havin' dude with a hundred ones in his pocket and a half ounce of trash dope in his mama's house Daddy."

"Cuz they fuckin' for three days!" Sage laughed. "Sounds like a wack, self-published, hood book scene."

She shook her head and reverted to her original thought. "Carlos Garcia… Mom told me they call him *Bienvenidos*. He's bigger than Duarte in the eyes of every wannabe Pablo Escobar in the D.R."

"*Duarte?*" he asked, puzzled.

"Oh. January 26 is Duarte's Day. He's the father of the country," she quipped. "Or Pico Duarte the mountain. 10,417 feet or 3175 meters – right here."

She showed him on her iPhone.

He put the phone back on top of the shelf before saying. "*Bienvenidos*. Welcome. Why they nickname him that?"

"He's a welcome sight," she murmured, feeling Sage's swollen length against her buttocks under the hot water. She maneuvered her open crack until her little bald cunt lips sat against him. Ever since he said he'd allow her to suck the dick of another man and watch her be pleasured and boned in the ass, her nipples were hard, her clitoris was pulsating, and her pussy was hungry for new cock. She quietly wondered who the guy would be, what his sperm would taste like, would he be hairy, how big his cock would be, and his balls. She loved real big balls and she had this thing with men's anuses. Sage had acted so weird with her for a long time. She had to "bang it into his head" that she was a fucking *girl* and that a man was not a homo for letting his girl get her freak on with his ass. Liza had made it clear that she got off on Sage's foot fetish so it was some unfair and selfish stuff to not let her do her thing. Luckily, all that's behind them.

Liza had never had sexual intercourse with another man but before they'd officially gotten back together, she had had oral sex with two boys. Sage had said something about group sex or he would set up something with another man for her and she was so excited. However, she was too shy to bring it back up because the last thing she needed was to have her marriage knocked off its perfect foundation by her husband feeling that his sex wasn't good enough. If he wanted to spice up the sex she was with it. If not, she was with it. It would be nice but she actually was sexually satisfied.

However, what woman *wouldn't* take an exciting new sex romp with her husband's okay?

"A welcome sight to crackheads and dopefiends?" Sage reasoned.

"Wellll…" she drew out the word. "From what I heard he has people for that. Sort of like you. You own businesses. You set your wife up in a cash-makin' business. We have off-shore bank, this beach-front property the United State cannot take. Bienvenidos has many businesses on both sides of the island. Mostly bars and nightclubs."

They rinsed, dried off, applied lotion to each other, and started getting dressed. "I still wanna hear 'bout Bienvenidos," Sage said as he was alerted of Tate's arrival with a group of individuals he came with.

Liza heard it over speakerphone. "Noni and Deva! Yes!"

Sage smiled, putting on some expensive dark B.A.P.E denim shorts and a white New York Yankees T-shirt. His wife walked into her own closet still fully nude, not wanting to sweat from the steam-bath and bussing from Sage's big throbbing dick touching her asshole and pussy under water a minute ago.

She located a New York Yankees Summer dress with black stripes and the team name and logo on the front and back. She put on Lancôme's perfume and had her husband help her put on a Tiffany's tennis bracelet diamond stud earrings and a lady's Rolex.

"Ready?" he asked her. "You fucking gorgeous, baby."

"Mmhm." They exited the room. "Thank you. I feel it. I'm in love with my Papi, we havin' another baby, we away from New York so you can breathe! In Santo Domingo of all places, and you gon' give me a real wedding."

"I said that? I ain't say that shit."

She slapped the back of his head. "Keep playin', boy!" she laughed.

"Ow!" he reacted to the slap. "You a pregnant lady now. You can't be behavin' like no monkey on steroids!"

"I do what I want." She was laughing so hard. "*Monkey on steroids!*"

"You think cuz you one of them bad ass Spanish bitches…" he trailed off. "Aight. Wait 'til you say, '*Papi, all Lupé and my mama – the baby's comin'!*' I'ma have my Beats Headphones on full blast, listenin' to da *Urban Aint Dead* soundtracks bangin' out to DJ Rell or Elijah R. Freeman kickin' it…"

He had her, Lupé, and Elizabeth laughing. "The helicopter come?"

"They here now." Elizabeth walked out on the large front patio and held her hair down as two whirlybirds landed on the two helicopter pads. "They got two helicopters! I thought it was jus' Deuce, Tate, and my cousins!"

She had to shout over the thunderous **WHOOOP! -**

WHOOOP! - WHOOOP! – noises of the blades and engines of each aircraft. Liza had purchased a pair of BELL 429 helicopters from an estate auction. Each were worth $200k but she got them for $195k – a total steal since one of them were worth that much. As it stood at the present moment the Black Fern did not own one. They badly needed at least two once they were awarded dual citizenship in the D.R. Those applications were pending.

To own and operate aircraft, no matter how recreational, the government had rules that state owners and operators had to have special licensing. To obtain that licensing they had to apply online or by mail and then appear in person for a series of rigorous tests. The Dominican Republic's licensing process was not so dissimilar to those in the States.

Disembarking from the first helicopter first were the two Dominican pilots. Liza, Lilly, Elizabeth, - who was holding baby Isabel - Lupé, all saw Noni and Deva and hurried to greet them once the engines idled, the blades slowed to a stop, and the engines died. Sage observed. *Nice fuckin' helicopters,* he murmured. *Looks like the ones I was 'bout to get on back up north,* he thought as he turned off the sprinklers which were alongside the right side of the house where Lupé, Elizabeth, and Elicia Sales, Isabel's homeschool teacher, had a garden of various vegetables growing to teach Izzy horticulture. Isabel loved the sun and being outside. She was like any toddler her age: she thought she was a dog one day because of all the different objects she put in her mouth. If it was a burning coal or 50,000 volt wire she'd try it out. The next day, in the garden for instance, Isabel was Optimus Prime or Bumble Bee because she transformed into a pig-completely soaked in mud. Later in the night as she was bathed. Liza called Sage to come take a look at the bath water.

"Got-damn, Lil Mama! Ha ha!" Sage had laughed. "She even got mud in her panties, babe. W-T-F, man!"

And, Izzy, as goofy a child as she was, laughed with her father and repeated, "W-T-F, *Mam*," about fifty times until sleep took her out late night.

"*LOOK AT THIS PLACE! MY GOD!*" Noni squealed after she and her older sister, Deva, embraced Liza.

Noni Honoret-Garcia, now 23, was Deuce's fiancée, and Liza immediately noticed the beautiful rose gold ring and factory-made 2.5 – carat chocolate diamond. All the females stood in a cipher while a few of the housekeeping staff gave the pilots refreshments as they re-fueled. Having the aviation fuel on hand greatly reduced the transportation costs to and from The Black Fern. The helicopters soon left.

"I love him so much," Noni proclaimed as all of the women checked out the ring she had.

Elizabeth hugged her again and kissed her niece on her cheek. "Good for you, sobrina…" she looked around their circle at the other quiet ladies. "And who are your friends and this cute little boy?"

Deva made all of the introductions. "The little boy is Maseo Heighlon and somebody said he was two years old,"

Deva said jokingly as everyone stood outside looking out at the sea just after the sun disappeared.

"I'm *four*," the little guy corrected.

"These ladies are…well me and Noni may have crossed paths a coupla-few times cuz we all in the same *family* so to speak," Deva stated, managing each word that came out of her mouth very consciously.

"Amris Brazil Heighlon is my name and I'm Kaz's woman." She spoke out sharply, cutting past what she deduced was Deva's pre-scripted bullshit. "Maseo's my son. This is my cousin Sparkles. She's a R&B singer who goes by Charlotte Sparkles. She opened for Usher a few weeks ago in Houston. These are my best friends Vaynale Churchyard – we call her Vee - and this is BLUE Chapman."

Elizabeth introduced herself, Lupé, Lilly, Izzy, Elicia, and Daniela as she and her security detail arrived. The entire group started to walk towards the front entrance when suddenly all anyone saw were these little bare legs and bare feet, because Isabel was taking off but not before her Daddy caught her.

"Jesus Christ!" Sage was mad as hell.

Liza and Sage were scared to death of Isabel falling over that rocky mountain cliff to her death. The view was beautiful, the Caribbean Sea – it's bling-bling shiny waters during the day as the sun hit it and at night when the moon and stars reflected off of it. But even some spiders and snakes had beautiful, colorful markings on them, yet they were the deadliest venomous creatures.

Fencing was being put up. All of the materials were now at the Black Fern and the contractors would be starting at 6:00 AM and done in two days.

"Y'all the girls from G-Bop t-shirt store," Daniela mentioned after the scare.

"Not anymore," Amris stated in a sad, sullen voice. Her comment even got Sage's attention.

"Our company is paid dividends from that store," Sage revealed. "What's that mean?"

"We were robbed…well, *burglarized.* I'm talkin' total clean up, clean out," Amris reported as the house help lined the foyer and hallway outside the family room with luggage brought by Tate, Deuce, Noni, Deva, Amris, Blue, Vee, and Sparkle. "If that's not devastating enough my man is missing. Kaz, Cumba, *and* Ammo are gone."

"A couple of days ago there was an explosion," Sparkles added on. "Wiped out the whole building and the one next to it. The news said there were parts of the house a mile away. And they found the fire hydrant outside was two blocks away."

Sage was thinking about the slaughterhouse. But Liza pulled it up on the desktop Dell via Google Earth Maps and showed it to everybody. "I have this enhancement of image app… hold on… there it is. It doesn't always work."

"Put it up on the wall screen, Liza," Sage told her.

He sat down with his daughter, sitting in his lap. Once he saw it he no longer worried about the slaughterhouse, it was obliterated by not one but several deviously-planned C-4 bombs. But, before those bombs were detonated, there were 110 gallons of gasoline soaked throughout the slaughterhouse with 110 gallons of crude oil.

"Look, Amris, I'm very sorry for the store," Liza told her. "But... was anyone killed in the explosion?"

"My life. It's been up for two minutes and down for twenty-seven." She shrugged, trying to stay tough. "No one was killed but that shit was professional. The ATF came and said the perpetrators were hiding somethin' in that basement because oil was used."

"Oil?" Liza repeated.

"Crude oil like car oil," Blue elaborated. "Kaz, Cumba, Ammo missing... then car oil to cover up somethin' in our basement? What do you know about that basement, Sage? Tate knows nothing."

Lupé and Elizabeth were hearing an earful, and Sage didn't like the fact that these L.A. bitches were trying to blast on him in front of them. So he stood up from where he was sitting and put his daughter down.

"What basement, sweetheart? I know as much as you," Sage told Blue and looked at Amris. "Why you askin' me?"

"We appreciate you taking us up outta there witchu," Amris said to Tate, not realizing that Tate and a few killaz he knew had used their bomb-making knowledge and experience to turn that shop inside out, unearth the place, blew it all to hell, and left no loose ends. "But first Kaz, Cumba, and

Ammo… missing or whatever… but we know about you bein' the boss, And we-"

"Kaz, Cumba, and Ammo are hired assassins, baby," Sage said it snide-fully, chuckling as he held his hand out to Deuce. "Fill me back up, bro."

The brown-skinned lovely little 5 foot 5-inch woman felt like they all needed to stop talking as though they were being accusatory to these men. They had to be careful because they knew Sage would throw them off that cliff outside, chop them up, and feed them to the birds and sea creatures out there.

"Do you know what happened to Kaz?" Amris asked Sage in a more submissive tone.

"When I heard y'all ain't see him, I sent out a priority word for them to contact me. They did not." Sage shrugged. "They were on a small journey to handle personal business of their own and… that was all of it. You ain't hear nothin'?"

Amris showed Sage the bogus text that Sage had sent her, which he recalled sending to her through Kaz's phone:

Baby, my bad didn't call, the false text read from Kaz's cellphone which Sage had at that time it was sent. *Tte (Tate) wasn't here but we goin' da distance to get da merch correct. I hitchu when we touch O.T. (outta town). One.*

"Youse go to the cops?" Liza asked. "A missing person's report-cops prolly coulda pinpointed like where that call originated. The area and whatnot."

Amris just shook her head, exasperated. "What Imma tell 'em 'bout da merch part? We get our goods from online wholesalers or Chinese bootleggers down on East 28th & Broadway, South Street Seaport, or Canal Street. The only other merch is your merch."

Elizabeth took Lilly away from all that "grown folk talk." Lupé followed with Isabel who had fallen asleep on the sofa, burnt out.

"Look, y'all down wit us, we gotchu durin' happy times or rainy dayz." He shrugged it off like he didn't have a bother in the world. "Liza's my wife. Y'all know her?"

"Seen 'er," Amris stated tiredly.

"Well, she's pregnant," Sage revealed.

"WHAT?!!" Noni exclaimed. "You got no sistas, man, and you ain't fuckin' -. I should bust yo pimple!"

"We gotta do ya hair!" Deva told her.

"This is all *yours*, Liza?" Blue asked her as she and Vee were suddenly inspecting Liza's unbelievably long and thick hair.

"My goodness, Mami, *si*. Yeah," Liza said in her own sensual sexy way, immediately drawing the four black women in towards her.

"I just wanted to say I don't want her getting no anxiety, anger, stress, and depression," he told them. "Can y'all do that? Youse all work for my wife but no mental pressures."

Amris glanced at her crew. Then she looked dead at him and asked, "Will I ever see Kaz again?"

He had nothing to offer.

"*Hey!! Amris, right?*" Liza inquired standing up, towering

over the petite, lovely woman. "Are you *brainless?* The answer's *no!* You *won't!* They're *dead.* How? I'm a *woman.* The wife of the boss. I know *nothin'* of what the men do. I *do* know not to question *gangsters.*"

Sage, Tatem, Deuce, and Daniela left the room.

"Stay here a minute," Liza told Amris, Vee, Sparkle, Blue, and her cousins. "Don't move."

She returned several minutes. Liza had a black and white Fendi suitcase which she sat on top of the solid black Italian marble coffee table.

"Fidel! Maribel!" Liza shouted two of the housekeepers' names out. They came in from the room they occupied while they were working. Maribel was an Aunt to Fidel who was twenty-plus years old.

"Yes, Mrs. Liza?" Maribel inquired. "Dinner for the guests?"

"Yeah, package them food from the pantry, too," Liza told her. They had been erecting several prefab homes near Black Fern Lake, far away from the salt water of the sea. They were basic double-wide homes but they were very simple to erect and furnish. Liza explained this to the four women. "No one went shopping yet for the new houses by the lake. Once y'all leave from here, I'll have our housekeepers take y'all to your place. I think there are three houses by the lake maybe four. Each has two bathrooms and two bedrooms. Maybe the first night y'all wanna share one but we got hi-tech cameras, motion sensors, 24-7 armed security, you'll see."

Amris nodded, quietly observing Liza who was as beautiful as she was deadly. She had a narrow waist and an out of this world ass. Liza caught the pretty, brown-skinned former XXX-porno star checking her out, but it was a sly down the side of her summer dress that had the slit in it. Amris' eyes lingered on Liza's shapely leg and feet. Amris eyed her cute toes and glossy white color French tops.

Maribel got all the staff together before it got too late and boxed up enough food to stock the prefab homes' shelves and refrigerators. They were already furnished so all they needed was bedding.

"C'mon, we'll go with y'all," Liza stated when she heard Sage inside of the office-study bitching Tate and Deuce out about somethin' that had happened up New York.

"You made me head of security!" Tate shouted.

"That doesn't mean *wholesale* murder, son!" Sage shouted back.

They had sent Daniela out of the meeting. She walked outside and saw several four-wheel all-terrain vehicles taking off towards the lake homes as Liza had ordered. A pick-up truck was loaded up as well. The housekeeping staff took care of the chore within an hour or so. It just wasn't a whole lot to do. Daniela, Elizabeth, and Lilly went over there with them, carrying all that they could.

"You okay?" Liza asked Daniela.

The red head nodded. "Yeah, yeah… well." She shrugged.

They stood on the pier that went out over the lake. There

were only three double-wide prefab homes next to the lake, not four like Liza had originally thought.

"Ay, I may as well be the one who fills you in," Daniela said, pondering how or what her words would be. "I know the Bargains Galore business is your pet project and you don't wanna go back to New York."

They walked away from the snooping ears of Lupé, Lilly, and Elizabeth.

"This bein' your fourth month of pregnancy," Daniela continued.

"Yeah, I wanna get this property together, buy horses, grow fruit crops, like banana, mango, hairy mango, plantain, coconut," Liza mentioned. "Most off, keep Coldhearted alive. Bargains Galore will survive. I'll go treasure hunting, traveling to auctions, garage sales, police and federal auctions, antiques sales – I've fallen in love with that business. But right now, Daniela… not New York right now."

"I'm not trying to talk you in to *anything,* Mami," the Mexicana-Irish girl said with an abundance of hand-gesturing.

"Spit it out, Dani," Liza told her.

"Tanya's dead," Daniela informed her. "So's Juicy, Ava, Sonja, Alejandra, Shay, Joyce, Blue Eyez, Diamond Girl, Black Barbie, and all Savage Hoodz men."

Liza was staring at her with her mouth open.

CHAPTER SEVEN

Illegal Drug Thugs
Taizhan and Claudia
Pelham, New Yor

I n New York, an ocean blue Lamborghini Hurcacán EVO with black smoke tint, matching interior, rumbled to a slow stop inside the Sunoco Gas Station & Mini Mart on Gun Hill Road, but it wasn't there to buy fuel. It parked near the bathroom; the young lady inside of it backed into the vacant *"DO NOT PARK HERE!"* space and waited.

She was nervous. Well, not exactly nervous. More like *paranoid,* which was almost the same except that "nervous" implied that nerves were jumpy and unsettled. Paranoid was more psychological where a person can believe she or he was being stared at, judged, or something when they're really not. Or she might think she was being followed when it's only a figment of her imagination.

This was the Boogie Down Bronx in broad daylight. 1:00 o'clock pm. Taizhan had every right to be paranoid, nervous – all that shit – because she had been arrested when she landed in Corpus Christi, Texas. A DEA agent recognized her "Blood Gang" tattoos during the flight and ran her name. *Taizhan Ivie Hooks.*

Her name did not stand out in the DEA database, or anyone else's for that matter, but when her address came back to Mt. Vernon, New York, the agent was wise and gung-ho enough to call the Mt. Vernon Police Department's Narcotics and Gang Units. Lieutenant Blackstone of the Westchester County Municipal Drug Task Force got the call. In about ten minutes she was emailing the agent the following communique:

WE HAVE FACTUAL INFO THAT MISS HOOKS RUNS THE MONEY TO Texas. A huge amount of illicit drug money from our Westchester borough and Bronx, New York City, for her boyfriend - street name Bugout - and the big Blood Gang Chicago boss 'P-Man' (we believe his name is Philip, but the 'P' means 'Piru' – a Blood gang). We've seen the acronym 'PIMPS IN RED' UNIFORMS written in red graffiti paint here in the city.

But we are thusly aware of the 'Piru Street' origins in Compton City, California.

THE DEA HAD FOUND A QUARTER MILLION DOLLARS IN suspected illegal drug proceeds that were packed inside of her luggage during a personal search when they'd landed at the airport. The DEA had technology that detected the presence of heroin, fentanyl, and/or cocaine. For the DEA, there was no big case to prosecute her on at that point except for the confiscation of the money as suspected drug money. As she'd sat inside of the TSA lock-up the agent had consulted with the DEA Field Chief.

Inside of Taizhan's purse was a key to a local storage facility. The DEA had waited for a search warrant to clear and subsequently entered the storage unit where they located a black Mercedes. They got permission to enter and search the vehicle. There, they had found three kilos of fentanyl pills and ten bricks of cocaine. Taizhan had found herself in deep shit.

The arresting DEA Agent who'd been on her American Airlines flight had disappeared from the picture. In his place two muscular men who wore black tactical pants, T-shirts, and Kevlar vests had entered the room where Taizhan was being detained. They'd had on black ski-masks with red lining around the eye holes like Spider-Man masks.

"We're not gonna fuck around with you, Hooks," one of them had said. It wasn't some bulljive good-cop bad-cop routine. These were those Donald Trump-era Texas-Mexican border mercenaries out there late at night shooting migrants and making sure they were never found. No graves... definitely no mass graves. Not when law enforcement now had a gadget that can see a fucking rotting corpse or bones through solid concrete. Yeah. So any motherfucker who thought he (or she) was smarter than a cop might be. But he won't outsmart some machine that can locate a buried body through that concrete!

Taizhan had nodded. "I know I'm fucked... Can I have a napkin with this sandwich they gave -"

The other man, who was black and a little taller than his partner, stood up, walked around the desk, and slapped the hoagie out of her hand so hard, it broke her fingernail. The sandwich went flying up against the wall.

"You think I'm runnin' a restaurant?!" he shouted at her.

"Ow! Ow! No! No, I don't, fuck!" she exclaimed as she held her thumb and forefingers. "I was... nothin'."

"Lemme tell you somethin'," the black man stated. "You're **nobody** to us. We chase cartel leaders, assassins, smugglers, men who're raping eleven-year olds at night and attending his daughters, grand-daughters, or nieces' *quinceañera.*"

"Speakin' of luck," the other agent cut back in. "Our A.U.S.A says we have the authority to cut you loose – *if you play ball.*"

With that, the hardcore "mercenary DEA, FBI, Homeland

Security agent" or whatever type of fucking agents these Texas assholes were… the narcotics were placed on her left and over to the right had been the keys to the black Mercedes-Benz. She started crying and shaking.

"We don't give a scorpion's ass 'bout those tears nor that manipulating female lying bullshit you all are good for," the shorter man growled at her and stood up. "That's it. You're under arrest for possession, conspiracy, interstate trafficking of narcotics, RICO ACT. Let's go."

"WAIT A MINUTE!!" she screamed at the top of her lungs. "Just *wait!* Wait… w-what I gotta do?"

The black agent uncuffed her and had her to write out a confession of what she was doing with the money, whose money it was, who her boss was, who their Texas contact was, and so forth. Taizhan discovered how far the feds would go to try and take out the man sitting at the top. These guys were heartless, they wanted to take out the buyers, the middlemen, users, and suppliers in one big raid. All it took was for one rat to knock down the entire empire and Taizhan was a fat slimy one.

She had been given the cashback, which she'd take to P-Man's longtime narcotic plug, Rooster, a Mexican MS-13 who owned a motorcycle sales and repair store in Corpus Christi. His father was a cartel associate in the Juarez Cartel with a base out of Matamoros. Hidden inside of the bag that held the money was a GPS tracking device. The bag sat inside of the motorcycle dealership for almost the entire time it had taken

Taizhan to drive the Mercedes, loaded with narcotics, back up to New York where she had turned over the keys to one of Bugout's people down on Southern Boulevard in the Bronx.

"You late!" was all he hissed at her before he went back inside of the nice loft apartment building.

It wasn't until the next day, at 1:00 PM when the beautiful Jamaican-Chinese girl had driven up into the Sunoco gas station inside of her flashy Lambo and parked it.

Doors down and locked.

Windows up, waiting.

But she didn't have to wait long.

A black Chevrolet Camaro, 1100 horsepower, Stage II Yenko/SC, rolled to a stop next to her, and down the windows went.

"Lieutenant Blackstone," Taizhan said to the brunette narcotics officer with light brown eyes.

"What this? Are you *trying* to commit suicide?!" Claudia Blackstone of the Westchester County Municipal Drug Task Force asked. "This flashy fucking machine? Follow me!"

Claudia drove to a business section of Pelham - that was a stone's throw away from Mt. Vernon - and made a turn into an underground garage. Taizhan was told to get inside of the Camaro. Claudia hit a button, and her butterfly door rose with an almost silent soft sound as the electronic hydraulic system inside of the Lamborghini door lifted it open. She sat inside of the hot new Camaro with the high-powered Yenko SC – supercharged – engine. As lieutenant of Westchester's drug task force, Claudia had her pick of a wide array of confiscated vehicles from illegal drug thugs.

The snappy brunette cop got right to it. "Bugout and P-Man. We have different aliases for P-Man's real name."

"Philip Maxwell Case," Taizhan stated, shaking her head. "They gonna kill me. Y'all are gonna get me killed."

Claudia looked at the lovely woman. She was so beautiful that Claudia almost wavered. Taizhan had super-sexual powers that very few women had. She was hypnotizing to look at. Even worse sitting inside the car so close to her, smelling her sweetness was even more mesmerizing. She could get anybody horny in no time.

"So, I shall say fuck my career and maybe even my own freedom to feel sorry for you?" Blackstone stated more than she inquired. "Give you a plane ticket to New Zealand or Singapore? Forget about the orders I was given? For what?"

Taizhan turned to Blackstone, hoping to answer that last part of the string of questions. But she didn't get a chance because Blackstone kept going.

"I'm not falling for nothin' you got Tay – can I call you Tay?"

Taizhan shrugged. "Whateva, man."

"You lie to me, you'll die," Blackstone warned her. "I'll send P-Man everything and deliver you to him in the trunk of a stolen car. Okay? Understand?"

Taizhan nodded.

"You set that strip club boss up, didn't you?" she fired at Taizhan.

"I-" Taizhan stared a hole through Blackstone before answering, "Yeah – I set him for Bugout."

"Why?" Lieutenant Blackstone pressed her. "Why do that to a man who loved you? I read all of the police notes and reports."

Taizhan was wearing a cute blue leather dress skirt, black blouse, and leather jacket with black knee length boots. "I never wanted to do that. I loved him, too. I was forced to do that."

"I'm s'posed to believe that?" Blackstone asked her, shaking her head and scoffing with the force of God's judgment at the lovely light skinned girl with the gray Chinese eyes. "Well, you better be lucky that I don't care much about the deaths of people who sell drugs to kids and pregnant females. I've tried to revive babies who overdosed, I seen what crack babies and dope babies look like, I also -"

Taizhan took off her jacket and lifted her silk blouse up from the back.

"What are y-." But Blackstone got quiet when the Jamaican-Chinese girl turned to face the window of the Camaro's passenger door. Red, black, and purple bruises covered her back about 60-65%.

Taizhan pulled her shirt down and put the seat back into a "rest" position. Blackstone watched as Taizhan pulled her skirt up past the point where her black G-string was.

Although she had many tattoos the officer could see the marks, some were scabbed over others were old. Blackstone leaned over for a closer look, and she didn't want to but she also breathed in Taizhan's sweet scent. It wasn't the scent of a *turned-on* woman but the warm smell of clean, soft female flesh.

"Goddamnit, Hooks," Blackstone said, sitting upright, deeply exhaling as she did so. "Those are cigar and cigarette burns."

"I didn't pick up my life," Taizhan told her. "A life of drug running for kingpins. I wanted a cute boyfriend, to be married, and not have to worry about money. Bugout promised me that but he's a gross animal."

Blackstone had seen it all before. "Well, all the more reason you have to help us get him off the street."

"These guys *own* cops," Taizhan commented. "I've had to have sex with all of them – blow your mind great sex. Two assistant district attorneys and a judge, too."

"Whattaya mean, *'had to have sex,'* Tay? With those D.A.'s and the judge? In Mount Vernon?" Blackstone asked.

Taizhan explained to her how she was not just beaten by Bugout but in some crazy way, she deserved it. And how her orgasms were so much more explosive.

"No, no, no, no, Tay!" Blackstone was passionately shaking her head and punching the horn hard. "Are you a fuckin' retard? He's controlling you with sex. He weaponized his dick! He's not the only fuckin' man with a good dick. Let me revise that: He's not the only man with a dick that's good to *you!* Jesus *Christ!*"

"How long do I have to work for y'all?" Taizhan wanted to know.

"*Y'all*? There's no 'y'all'. It's just MVPD now. However, if you renege, your case reopens with the DEA and back to the wolves you go. They have bigger fish to fry. But – and that's a BIG but – they want Bugout and P-Man's connections in Mexico which they're workin' on without getting you killed as the rat. And believe you me, they are wasting no time coming down on the bastards who loaded you up with those keys of fentanyl and cocaine."

Claudia opened up her purse.

"A cop with a Birkin? That bag you have, I don't even think Beyoncé has one yet," Taizhan mentioned as she closely observed the expensive bag the undercover taskforce detective had.

"You know what this is?" Claudia held up a make-up box.

"Yeah, a *Fenty* Make-Up Case with a mirror by Rihanna," Taizhan said.

"Doesn't she have my Birkin bag yet?" Claudia's smile was as equally sarcastic as her question was.

"Beyoncé has a person team who post nearly everything on her social media to feed her millions of fans, the *BBE-HIVE,*" Taizhan told her. "Rihanna has the same. The Birkin bag in question, RiRi has three of them."

Claudia used a stainless steel nail file to pop the box open.

"It's a microphone and a camera. This one is appropriate for the bedroom where you can place it on top of the dresser. This one…"

Taizhan's nerves were already fired from the arrest in Texas. "You fuckin' people. There's no bridge you won't burn… no earth you won't scorch, huh?"

Claudia opened up the box to the long rectangular electronic device inside. "You know nothing."

She found a small tool kit inside of the glove compartment and took a small Philip's screwdriver out of it. She used it to open up the "*surge protector*." Then, from inside of a pouch on her cellphone cover, she produced an S.I.M. card.

"You plant this right here… like so, and I can call from anywhere around the world and hear whatever's being said for ten feet," she told Taizhan.

"That's some top spy shit," Taizhan responded to what she was seeing.

"All you need to do is plug it up in the living room area or home office where he does his talking and I promise you, when we get him, he'll never get out of prison again," the officer told her.

Taizhan nodded, fear in her face.

"Simple instructions. The Make-Up Case eye faces where y'all sleep and talk," Claudia reminded her informant. "We need to feed the DEA in Texas more information ASAP."

"Stop at Walmart," Claudia also explained to her. "This way that psychopath boyfriend of yours won't suspect anything if you or when you enter the house with bags. And for God's sake lose the receipt."

"That audio-visual make-up box… you're gonna see a lot more than two people talking." Taizhan stated in a low voice.

Claudia paused. "I'll see it. No one else… except the pertinent pieces of audio."

Taizhan got out of the car, taking the items with her. She put them into the passenger seat, "Hey, Blackstone."

Taizhan walked around to where the lieutenant sat behind the wheel. "Yeah?" The officer asked. "What is it?"

"Will you masturbate when I fuck him tonight?" she asked in a sensual manner while watching Claudia's full pink lips parts a little bit at the raunchiness that came from the sexy black and Chinese girl. "I am. I know I am. When I let him fuck me doggy-style I'll look right at you, reach my hand under me, and play with my clitoris just for *you*." Standing there, she removed her G-string and gave it to the cop. "Here. I can tell when another woman wants my cunt. Smell it when you masturbate tonight, okay? And if you're not scared next time let's fuck each other."

Claudia watched the sexy girl get into her car and leave, not believing all the nasty things she'd just said to her. Claudia tossed the G-string panties out of the Camaro's window and started the car.

"Whore!" Claudia cursed. Starting to pull off, she barely drove forward three feet before she hit the brakes, parked, and got out of the car. She retrieved the panties and got back into the car where she closed her eyes, deeply sniffed the lovely musky scent of Taizhan's pussy and whatever body spray or perfume she'd applied after her morning shower.

"Claudia, Claudia, *Claudia!!!*" she whispered. "First, Sage Thomas… now lusting after one of the Blood Gang's top drug and money smuggling girls? Fuhgeddaboudit!"

She had taken a snapshot of the Lamborghini with her cell-phone and noted the license plate number on the high-end luxury vehicle as well. She immediately drove back to Task Force HQ to write up a "Supplemental Report" for the case code-named: *SPARKSFLY.* What the term meant she did not know. All Claudia Blackstone knew was she had to do her part in the *sparksfly* investigation.

CHAPTER EIGHT

"Liza Understood"
Black Fern Beach, D.R.
12:50 PM (Noon)

"You got a lighter anywhere?" Tate asked Sage after drying himself off. He had just come back from a swim in the clear blue waters of the Caribbean Sea. He had rolled several small sticks mixed with the stuff he liked to get on with.

It was only Coldhearted, Tate, Double Deuce, and Liza on the shore of the white sandy beaches of Monte Cristi. The cat was completely out of the bag now. Sage was telling his wife his thoughts on everything as he laid out underneath the huge colorful umbrella on the large blankets they had spread out there earlier.

"He's *H.O.S.,*" Sage shrugged coldly, passing Tate a lighter. "What's in them pieces?"

Tate lit the blunt paper-wrapped joint up. "That *designer,* nigga: O.G. Kush, a lil K-2, and Angel Dust – PCP."

Sage accepted a few pulls and it hit him with a really nice high. "Fuck you lookin' at, bitch?" he laughed at Liza.

Liza shook her head. "Wit Tanya out the way, she can't blow no whistle 'bout Chubb, but that blew a hole right through what I had set up wit Bargains Galore."

She was without a question pissed off with Tate but she understood.

"I know, bae... but if she ain't get chopped..." Sage shrugged, knocked the ash off of the joint and passed it to Deuce who declined. Tate took it back.

"Ayo, lil sis..." Tate searched for the right words. "If she wasn't chopped she woulda called 9-1-1 to look for Chubby. And he was tryna play double agent."

"I thought he was crossin' da enemy," Liza discussed the fact of why Chubby got hit. "I thought he said he was impatient of why nobody got bopped for Rock getting' slumped. So, he started feeding the cops information about Bugout and his clan."

"Babe, that's what he wanted us to believe," Sage informed her. "We couldn't trust a nigga on da team who snitches on *anybody.* Too risky."

Just then, they heard the sounds of thunder real low in the distance. "Look!" Tate pointed and Liza rose to her feet. Deuce and Tate couldn't help but sneak clandestine glances at her fabulous big and delicious sun-tanned and honey brown booty-cheeks. Sage knew that his wife's ass was impossible for people not to look at.

Liza squealed and put on her white sarong to give her lower ends a modest cover. "The horses! Los cabayos, Papi!"

"These are yours?" Tate asked no one in particular.

Sage nodded. "Yeah. I don't know how to ride but… I like 'em. My wife wanted them."

Deva, Noni, Double J, Spooky, and Amris were all on horseback. The horses were among a herd that were purchased for The Black Fern Ranch. Liza had been setting their ranch up to make money and having horses on the vast property was necessary and occupational not just recreational. Most of them were three-year old Quarter Horses and others were Appaloosas.

"Beautiful. Just beautiful. Look at Lilly and Amris, Daddy," Liza whispered as Lilly came trotting down the beach with cowgirl boots, jeans, hat, and the entire get-upon.

Seconds later, Vee, Blue, and Sparkle rode down the edge of the water line with three of the ranches Raptor 660 4-whell all-terrain motor vehicles. Sage watched Amris. She looked much better.

"Bae," Sage said as they watched everyone have fun.

"Hm?" Liza answered.

"Amris and her girls… that's ya Bargains Galore movement right there," Sage suggested. "I love the idea of the D.R. bein' our Home Number Two. But New York is Home Number one. Am I right?"

Liza nodded.

"No reason you can't have the B.G. website built up and runnin' hard twenty-four seven, three sixty-five," he told her. "We got a buyer for Garters, a real serious buyer. And we got offers under the askin' price for the house. One is $1.8, the other $1.9 mil."

They walked back to the house, feeding seagulls along the way. Sage carried a modified AR-15 machine gun with a Velcro shoulder strap. As they neared the house Liza said, "You look sexy carrying that thing. Lemme shoot it."

He grinned and gave it to her. "Just shoot it. Aim it out at the sea."

They stood at the newly-built fence –between the swimming pool, perimeter fence and cliffside with the 100-foot drop to the beach below. She aimed out over the sea and let loose. ***BB-RR-AAA-TTT!!! BB-RR-AAA-TTT!!!*** That motherfucker had a crazy kick. She had it sounding like "44 Minutes" in North Hollywood when them white boys blasted on those LAPD pigs.

"This a cop killer, Papi?" she asked.

"NYPD got 2-2-3 ammo now," her husband said, taking the gun back. "So they can fight us off. It's too even of a fight. When we say *'cop killas'* niggas mean shit like the M249

S.A.W. or Squad Automatic Weapon. It can be fitted with a bi-pod and collapsible buttstock that allows for blasting in extended and collapsed positions and a shorter barrel for movin' around in close-quarter combat."

"Like in a crackhouse," she said as they entered the house, making Sage laugh but nod in the affirmative.

Isabel was soaking wet with bubbles from the bathtub. Elicia and Maribel were hot on her tail.

"Jesus Christ," Sage said while scooping her up, and handing Izzy back to Elicia.

Sage and Liza could only get Izzy to take a nap if someone slept with her. Sage was happy to go to sleep for a little while because he knew that he was going to finally go out and go hard later. He had to. They were going to meet Bienvenidos, Liza's father, Carlos Juan Jaramillo-Garcia.

And island bigwig.

Sage wondered how big.

CHAPTER NINE

"Stretch my pussy!"
Black Fern Lake Orgy
12:25 Midnight

T he rain came down out of nowhere and it came hard. They were all supposed to go out that night, but it was just common sense to scrap those plans due to all of the flash floods raking through the country at the time. They weren't calling it a hurricane. Oh, the northeast coast. What's known as Samaná Peninsula was part beach resort, part hippie enclave, and probably one of the most beautiful places on the entire island. One of the remarkable things about this particular area was that it's where humpback whales migrated between January and March to give birth.

All night, Liza and Sage were looking at the path of the big storm on an iPad. "This fucker's comin' our way. See? I thought it'd be just rain for a minute but goddamn." Sage showed his wife.

They were in the living room at the moment. That's when she told him about the humpbacks. "Well, rain storms pop up and sometimes they come big, Papi. I'm goin' to check on the horses."

"No wonder it's a steel barn. Now I get it." He got dressed with her. "You ready?"

She grabbed a key ring and on the way out. Sage spoke with an armed security guard named Franco who nodded his head and made his way in the opposite direction from where Liza and Sage were headed. She asked about the security personnel and where Sage had sent him.

"To make sure Sparkles, Vee, and all of them is okay," he told her.

She held a big bag of apples which she carried as the rain hit them in a sideways cascade. It was still warm out but it had cooled from the 86 degrees humid heat from earlier. Their rain jackets did very little to help keep them from getting wet. They ran the rest of the way to the massive stable where all of the horses were being kept.

There were already two men and two women there. Sage was still trying to wrap his mind around the fact that he let

Liza purchase The Black Fern Ranch. Not only that but it was a fully-functioning ranch with a staff already. Liza had the genes to create income out of horse-trading and selling, tropical fruits and vegetable farming for the local markets – things like that.

"No way we can't make land like this create hundreds of millions of dollars one day," Liza had sworn up and down. And when her mother and Lupé finally saw it they – breathlessly – both had agreed.

"It's a dream, Daddy. All Latinos dream of havin' way smaller land than Black Fern. Take the blood money and create jobs for hairy mango growers, mango growers, orange growers, strawberries, cumquat, yucca, plantain, grow our own hay… Daddy, it's over three thousand acres. My heart beats so hard about Black Fern, not just because Liza loves money, but we can feed hungry people. *Us,* who did all this dirty bloody stuff to get Black Fern."

"We? No mama. Let me carry that guilt. *Me,*" Sage whispered in his fierce, protective way over his angel baby. "You innocent and *perfect* and *good.* You can never do wrong or be wrong. Not in my eyes. You my mama. Always been my mama."

She loved him so much but deep down she knew she'd be in hell with him one day.

"Who're y'all again?" Sage asked the two females. One was brown-skinned with an Afro-curl. The other one looked almost like a white woman.

"Valentine Larrichia," the white-looking woman said in clean English. "I'm your supervising horse veterinarian."

"American?" he asked her.

"Yes sir, we're from the Universidad de Nacíonal. I've been there for six years," the blond woman explained. "To help the Dominican economy you'll find a small army of American students studying classes that'd be accepted credits in USA college programs."

He met the other veterinarian assistants. "Okay, c'mon babe. Let's feed 'em snacks."

They gave the beautiful animals the apples first. Then Liza showed him how to ride one of the male quarter-horses. He saddled her up first and hopped on. He instantly liked it and had an idea.

"Good boy!" Sage said, patting the big brown horse on the neck. "C'mon, Mommie."

Liza put a hand on her hip and smiled as if she was thinking about it first. "This is not goin' to end well," she teased him with a laugh.

Valentine Larrichia helped her up with a step stool and a firm grip around her right arm. "You're pregnant so be careful, Mrs. Garcia-Thomas."

"How'd you know?" Liza inquired. "Am I showing?"

"No. Not yet anyhow. But…" Larrichia shrugged. "All the staff knows. Be careful out there."

"You're comin' with us," Liza ordered.

"Yes, ma'am." Larrichia saddled up a white Appaloosa mare, threw on a raincoat with rubber boots, and followed the couple outside. "There's flash floods from Samaná Bay to Cabarete. Puerto Plata is getting hit right now but not a lot of wind."

Puerto Plata was considered the Dominican Republic's best when it came to its many beach resorts. Monte Cristi was in the Puerto Plata region, but they were clearly different cities. Puerto Plata was located next to Mount Isabel de Torres. Monte Cristi was nearly 50 miles to the east – close to the Haitian border.

Liza rode in front, and Sage sat behind her, urging his woman to show him how to ride. "Pulling him left, he'll go left, Papi. Right, he'll go right. Pulling *lightly* back on both reins slowly to stop him. Pull further back, he'll walk in reverse. Be easy on the reins. There's a bit in his mouth."

He learned quickly. They went to Black Fern Lake where the pre-fabricated houses were being occupied. All except two of them. There were six of them out there now. Sage stopped their horse in front of one of the unoccupied but fully-furnished homes and they got down off the big animal.

"We gon' stay down here," Sage told Valentine Larrichia. "Take him back up for us."

Valentine said good night and took the horse back to the steel stable and barn. "We never stayed down by lake, bae. What are you up to?" Liza asked as he took her down to the pier on the large almost oval shaped lake. "It's still raining."

"Yeah but it's like seventy degrees and raining," he pointed out. "That's unheard of in New York."

"W-e-e-lll…almost," Liza said as he took her hand and pulled her with him to the wooden benches in the center of the pier. It was the only place around the lake that offered a little shelter because it was high-backed smooth wooden bench made out of cedar and there was a cover over it.

"This is cool," she said as they sat down and listened to the rain fall on top of it and out on the top of the lake, making the water look like it was boiling or simmering or something. The only light was from the yellow-white lamps on the pier which were low voltage fluorescent lights that came on and off from an automatic timer. "It's beautiful."

He looked at her.

She smiled at him. "Out *here*?" She knew what he was thinking.

"You don't want to?" he asked.

She scoffed in that cute sucking her teeth type of way that he liked. "My clit just popped out that soft little blanket she sleeps in the second you looked at me like that."

He didn't hesitate after hearing how she said that hot shit. He kissed her slowly for a second but then her eagerness hit him and he just devoured her candy lips and fruit-juicy tongue. She was one of these Spanish girls that wanted her mouth to feel fucked like the rest of her horny parts. So he wanted all of her sloppy saliva.

"Spit in my mouth," he breathed while holding her wet face and hair in his big hands.

She didn't think at all, she just did it. He opened his mouth and she spit, and he licked his tongue slowly around his wet pretty lips and swallowed. Then he stood up and slowly stripped in the rain for his baby. His *bambina.* She was laughing and staring at every inch of his godlike body.

"We gon' get caught!" she whispered.

"Don't we own it?" he asked her, his bone looking swollen and pumping blood through all of it enormous pulsating veins.

"Damn your dick looks wild with raindrops on it," she murmured as he then stood her up and took all of her clothes off. He made sure all of their stuff was on the bench, "Damn, I-ummm, oh, Sage… we should…"

He sat down and sucked on her gorgeous nipples. Hard little missiles. He spread her legs and grabbed her big lovely ass from underneath. He kept thinking about the promise he'd made to her and allow another man to fuck her in her phat ass. That ass that even some straight women lusted over and envied her for.

"You know Daddy loves you?" he said as she spread her slick wet pussy slime against his giant cockhead and she whimpered at the pleasurable contact.

She was already very turned on. He could tell that she was hot from the buttery heat he felt from the inner pinkness of her soft rose opening up and spilling her cream as she pushed and slid that pussy along the stiff upper ridge of his long cock. "Oh god yes… I do you sexy fucker!" she breathed into his ear. "Get… it… in. In. In. Innnn meeeee, ohh shit… I love this long and thick shit… so wide. Stretch my pussy! Fuck iiittt!"

He was deep up in it now and she was riding it. Up. Down. Up. Down. Staring into his face and then feeding her beautiful titties to her man. Sage loved these fleshy orbs. She emitted sweet sighs that stole his heart. Women knew that men loved the moans but it was the less subtle noises that they never knew men paid most attention to. Liza yelped and a delicious mini-cum hit her surprisingly hard.

"Um! Ohh! Sage, I know you love me! I know!" She was crying real salty tears. Real good orgasms busted holes in her tear ducts. He loved that shit. It was weird but he loved it.

As men knew when he tapped that ass like Sage did Liza's, he knew she'd travel to Iran, feed the Ayatollah Khomeni pork fried rice, talk him into butt-fucking Benjamin Netanyahu, and shoot both of them dumb bastards in their guts if Sage wanted her to. Liza could never explain it but Sage had magic all in his dick. And vice versa. Liza was really the only woman in the world for Sage.

"You gon' be okay." He wrapped his arms around her and for whatever reason, he cried with her. And it astounded her because that had never happened. He was such a *"man's man"* like Aniello Dellacroce (AKA "Neil") of the infamous Gambino Crime Family used to say about mobster John Gotti. *UrbanAintDead.com,* the publishing company, had a riveting 3-book series coming out entitled: *The Black Gambinos: A*

John Gotti Hood Tale by Lou Garden Price, SR. and Jadaysia Borrerro.

She grabbed his face and stared into his eyes and the only thing she saw was a husband who loved her and who'd finally allowed the true and raw emotion for her, himself, and their new baby to blossom. It was a moment she'd never forget. She saw the sensitivity of a toddler inside of him and it made her a different woman.

He picked her up, cradling her, and not thinking, jumped off the pier into Black Fern Lake.

"I knew you was gonna do that! I knew it!" she exclaimed but her face was beaming. She blew her nose and rinsed it.

He swam to the stairs instead of the boat launch. "Uhn-uhn, ma. It's slippery and dirty over there."

She swam to him. "You slippery and dirty," she wise-cracked.

Back on the bench they grabbed their clothes and walked on to the pre-fabricated home. The front door was open. They entered and went to the bedroom. It was a nice Queen-sized bed in there, Liza pulled the covers back and jumped right in. Sage came from the bathroom moments later and then he went up front. He came back with drinks and other refreshments.

"Astroglide? I'm not even gonna ask how this got here," she stated as she grabbed the bottle of lubricant.

He smiled impishly. "Not me. I'm a faithful husband. We honest in this marriage cuz we best friends. And don't forget we are legally cousins."

That made her bust out laughing. "Oh my goodness… c'mere." She crooked her index finger, spread those phat ass thighs, bowed her little feet. "Come kiss your cousin… on both sets of lips. Tell me which ones are softer… wetter… taste better… smells better…"

"Damn!" Her clit was hard, swollen, and eager. "Happy Birthday, baby."

He dimmed the lights. "That's what this is?" she asked, fingering her juicing cunt.

He got onto the bed from the foot end and dove into her Puerto Rican-Dominican paradise. She pulled his face against her sweet sex. She knew that what she had was special and unique. He grabbed her wet ass and she pulled on his ears as her hips started to swirl in circles around his lips and tongue. She hampered her little bald pussy up and down in his face.

"You gon' fuckin' make me buss this honey all in… Sage! Daddy!" she whimpered out.

"Um, unn, I love dis pussy-soft juicy shit!" he blurted, looking up at her as she pulled on her breasts and pinched on her nipples.

Just as she was about to cum he stopped and moved to the left. "What da fuck -? I was about to cu -."

"Meet Franco, Mommie," Sage suddenly said as the security man walked in. He was not as tall as Sage but he was 5 feet 11 inches and sexier than all the boys on the last season of "*FB*" and "*Paradise Island*" put together. He stood in the doorway staring at her with his light gray eyes, a towel wrapped around his center, and as their eyes locked, his cock grew and grew and Liza's lips were stuck open from the shock of it. She pulled the pillow between her legs, unsure.

"Hi, Liza, you're…" he looked at Sage who sat in the chair next to the bed. "You may have seen me around the last few days. I'm Franco. A dancer and adult entertainer."

Suddenly, she smiled. "You really planned this for my birthday? A stripper?" Sage only smiled. "Thank you. You sure 'bout this?"

"Bae," he nudged her. "How many times we share a bitch?"

Franco dropped the towel and Liza's mouth watered. He got between her legs, gently pulled the pillow away from her, and placed it underneath her. "You have the body of perfection, Liza. And the name is from a Goddess."

He sucked her clitoris softly, teasingly. The way she started to hump and fuck his mouth meant that he was all over the bullseye. Her eyes were closed at first and then open. She cried out loudly, her long thick hair tossing hard as she came. Sage had thought he'd want to kill the motherfucker for touching his wife but seeing her naked sex was mind-blowing. And his dick was harder than a diamond cutter right now.

"I'm gon' watch him fuck you, baby. You want his big dick inside you?" Sage asked, getting back on the bed where she wanted him.

"In my ass right?" she asked, reaching down past her

drippy cunt and touching her anus. "Franco… you like my little asshole?"

"My fuckin' god you're hot!" Franco said. He clutched her slim ankles and stared at her feet. "Pretty feet. You like havin' your toes sucked?"

"Nobody touches her toes, kid," Sage warned him.

Franco nodded.

"No toes and no tongue kissin'," Sage warned him.

Franco understood. He draped her thighs over his shoulders as he started tongue-slapping her clitoris all over again. He worked two then three fingers into her oozing pussy. This woman was special and much better than the women he was used to. Liza was rich, superbly clean, and a body to kill and die for. She had expensive tattoos all over her as if she was a model for *Go Virol, Bottlez & Modelz, Buttman* magazine, or something. She was a classy top-notch bitch like one that KITE MAGAZINE featured.

Franco spread that little pink cunt open and lapped all the mango juices and honey dripping out of her hairless asscrack and asshole that was in there. He shocked her sexy ass into another orgasm and before that one had dissipated she screamed out one more. Sage had never seen his wife climax so violently. Afterward, the sexy nude male dancer sat back on his knees and stroked his big lovely cock – balls and all. Baby girl panted hard, wiping the droplets of sweat from her forehead, and he caught her hand and licked all of her sweat from it.

"*Dios mio*. All of you taste good," Franco told her.

He bent down and kissed her lips. "No tongue, like the boss said. But other things?"

Liza nodded, wanting anything Franco had to give her.

Franco slid forward, rubbing his dick and balls all over her belly, moving up to where her big breasts were. She pushed them together and slowly, so slowly, he stroked his long length in and out. She grabbed his ass and stuck her tongue out to lick the sea-salty like corona which was the size of an egg. Then she let go of her breasts and his huge, thick cock slid inside. She kissed the pre-cummy dickhead and off to the left side of her cheek it went. He smelled like a man, different from Sage. She took him into her mouth and sucked. He fed her more and more of his big organ and her sucking became frantic.

Franco grunted and made animal noises. He bucked and she clutched really hard on his white buns as he spurted warm gobs of cum into her mouth. He pulled out of her and the sweat dripped down his muscular chest and eight-pack abdomen. She fell back with one hand across her breasts, the other thrust between her closed legs. She kept licking her lips, loving how another man's semen taste.

Franco was still hard so he stroked his strong manhood and looked at Liza. She turned to Sage who gently kissed her lips until the kiss got furious and wet as the two often do. She lowered her mouth to Sage's shaft, opening wide and taking about half of his meaty staff into her mouth, then she began sucking with a gusto, sliding her lips up to suck his fleshy knob before taking him back inside. Behind her, Franco laid her face down and matched her sucking on Sage for a while.

She spread her legs wide and Franco moved down between her legs. His warm breath teased her bald pussy. He spread her ass cheeks apart and blew on her pussy lips and asshole until she wanted to scream. And then his tongue was on her, proving every fold of her perfect genitalia and crevice. When he sucked her clit just right she jumped up, rising on her knees and pushing that beautiful ass out at him.

"Aight, Franco, if she says stop, stop," Sage told him, pushing her away.

Franco put Liza on her back and spread some of the Astro glide onto her pussy and anus below. He put two pillows up underneath her ass. She was confused. She thought that Sage didn't want any man to have her pussy, especially because of their baby. But she was so hot now and Franco's dick looked so good.

Liza opened her legs for him as the huge egg-sized head of his dick furrowed through her tiny loving cup. He positioned himself for maximum penetration, sliding his hands under her ass, talking nasty to her. He heaved forward and smoothly pushed it on home, burying himself until his balls fell over her anus. She whined out with sexy sounds of surprise and delight, returning each of his thrusts with one of her own. Soon the bed was shaking and banging against the wall as he hammered her wanton pussy.

"Sweet Liza!" Franco yelled, pulling out of her and reaching down. She reached down with him until the thick head popped inside of her asshole.

"Franco!! He's in my ass, Daddy!" she screamed, using one foot on the bed and the other he held locked on his back. She rammed her ass down onto his big pole and they rode it.

He fucked her deep, deep, deeper and never pulled a whole lot out. He loved her anus. The temperature was different in there or something. It was like a baby never wanting to be born. He fought like hell not to cum inside her. He was able to suck and bite and squeeze her titties. He turned her around and it was like Sage wasn't there. He was stroking his incredibly hard dick and swearing each second not to cum. He watched the male porn star buttfuck the hell out of his naked, pregnant wife while pinching her clitoris and finger banging her naughty cunt. Her hot bald pussy.

"Aaaaaarrrrgggghhhh, Fucccccckkkk ittttt. Liza. OOOOOOOOOOOHHHHHHH!!!" Franco screamed and bit her again.

She screamed and hollered, too. The sex was so hot, so wet, so juicy.

Sage let him out a little while later. Liza was too exhausted to do anything. However, as she lay there passed out, Sage couldn't help but to enter her sore, swollen pussy from missionary position. As he started to fuck her, she was still asleep but her horny body and cut came alive. She grabbed his ass, lifted her legs up and everything.

"Bae, you awake?" he asked her.

Liza was almost snoring in another world somewhere. But her pussy wanted dick. Her nipples were hard, standing up. Sage *had to* cum. He just had to after the last couple of hours of what Franco had given her. Sage spewed what felt like a cupful of cum inside of her and when he was done, he threw the soiled sheet on the floor. Then laid down next to her.

She snuggled up next to him. "Love you, Daddy," she whispered.

"Night, babe."

CHAPTER TEN

Franco's Head Fell
Black Fern Ranch, D.R.
4:47 PM

"Hey!" the woman's voice called out to him as he walked briskly through the muddy road towards the main house. "You that new security guy, huh?"

Franco, carrying an umbrella, wearing tan khakis and a black T-shirt, stopped and saw Amris holding a drink, standing on her front patio. There was an enclosed front deck built for her house because of Maseo, her son, needing the area to play at. So, there was a storm roof, furniture, even carpet inside the patio enclosure.

"Yeah, you're Amris, the other triple XXX star," Franco said with his Puerto Rican accent.

"You ain't Dominican, huhn?" she inquired.

He chuckled. "That's strange?"

"Kinda," she told him.

"Is everybody in the United States from the United States?" he stated back.

He turns to chuckle. She had on translucent nylon jogging shorts that were so tight that the prominent outline of her lightly hairy pussy could be seen so well that a sketch artist could draw it perfectly. "Okay," she said with a smile. "And I know I used to do Triple X work, and one of my friends did as well… but she was not a big name. So who's the 'other' Triple X star?"

"Never mind, my sweet," Franco waved her off.

"You wanna come in for a drink?" she asked him.

"Nobody sleeps around here?" He looked at his watch and right at that moment, Amris saw the stealth and the flash…

Franco's head fell to his left but Amris swore to God, in her mind, that he stood there, at the bottom of the four wooden steps leading into her patio enclosure, facing her for at least five seconds after his head was gone. He hit the ground backward.

Amris stared at the body, the blood geysering from vital "big" veins, namely the jugular vein because the heart was still pumping. "I read online that it does that because it has no brain to tell the heart that it's dead," she mentioned.

"Tell it den," Sage told her as he wiped *"Miss Heartless"* clean with a handkerchief. He sheathed it in the expensive Alligator skin scabbard, pocketed the hanky, and removed a black body bag from the backpack he carried. He picked up the head and placed it in there first. Then he rolled Franco's body in there while Amris disappeared inside the house.

She helped him carry the body around the side of the house where they covered it with a tarp from the barbeque pit and firewood. She had gotten dressed and together, they walked up to the main house. There they got one of the work trucks. There was an industrial-sized wood chipper next to the barn which they hitched it up to the new Chevy Silverado.

They drove back to Amris' house, picked up the body, and drove it down to the beach past the Wharf and Marina where La Liza Rosa/ The Liza Rosa was docked. Amris watched her boss strip to his boxers, remove Franco's body, and lay him out on the beach. There, Sage used his heavy machetes to chop the man's legs off, his arms, and then the rest of him.

"You need Jesus," Amris told Sage.

"If you gon' help be naked," he told her, laughing at the comment. "I don't but he does."

Amris stripped naked. She plugged the wood chipper up to the gas generator inside of the truck and using bare hands, they started to throw pieces of the man who had been paid to fuck his wife into the Caribbean. Parts of him were shot twenty yards or more out over the crashing waves. It didn't take long. When they were done they burned the body bag, and used buckets of seawater to wash the wood chipper and all evidence of blood.

It was also a great excuse to swim for a while. "I heard the stories," the beautiful former porn star and nude model said as she waded in the cool refreshing sea water. It was dawn out, the rain was all gone, and the skies were almost clear of clouds. "To see you move… wow. Women are turned on by hard, violent men. But you know that, huhn?"

He dipped his head under the water. "Yeah. I think so. C'mon. Before the sun comes up."

They got out of the water and he couldn't stop looking at her beautiful, phat, brown ass. He was so used to loving Liza, who was nearly white, that he deprived himself of all the other sweet brown and those insanely beautiful Ebony women. He chuckled to himself.

"What?" She looked at her forearm, stopping in front of the much taller Sage.

He felt his dick swelling up harder than a stick of dynamite. Putting both hands onto her tiny waist, he steered her toward the Silverado so she wouldn't keep looking down at his rapidly swelling man-piece. But he hit her in the back with it. He opened the passenger side door, got in, and sat up in the seat, his dick all out of control at the sexy visions of Liza sucking another man's big cock and hungrily swallowing his cum. Hundreds of hot and sticky visions. Her pussy being stretched open… her hot asshole taking that hot tool in her sweet Latina alabaster buns. He sat back, tired.

"Your dick looks like it's going to…" She climbed her little 5 foot 5-inch frame in between his legs, down on her knees on the floorboards, and took him inside of her mouth. Those Jennifer Hudson's lips that Kaz had described were now wrapped lustfully around his heated meat.

He opened his legs wider. "That's good, damn Amris… shit. Perfect, baby."

Amris put all of her porn star experience and passion into deep-throating and shallow-sucking him. She'd been wanting him. She pumped her pretty little head down and up while her hands helped.

"That your pussy getting all wet, Amris Brazil Heighlon?" he asked, which got him a moan and loud moan out of her. "C'mon, mama. Get up, baby. We gotta do it right and Imma fuck you right, okay? And you just gon' be my bitch. Ya heard?"

Amris nodded and he pulled her upward. "Kiss me, baby."

The 30-year old brown skinned beauty kissed him and stroked his cock. She was so horny that she was shaking and drool fell from her mouth. She turned and rubbed that phat brown ass in circles on him until the tip plopped inside of her soaking wet pussy. He wanted to push her off of him but his big hands and strong arms encircled her like a 16-foot 100 pound Bermuda python did the body of its prey. The way he squeezed those titties did something devilish to them both. Her slick, slippery, cunt bounced and squished. Up. Down. Up. Down. Up. Down.

He felt that grown woman pussy.

And the scent of a real grown Black woman's juicy turned on cunt was raw, earthy, and made a nigga need and come for more. And they knew what they were doing. Amris turned around and she took complete control of this fine young motherfucker. It smelled like her sweet pussy was a stream cloud all around them.

She opened the door back up and sobbed as huge rivulets of sweat cascaded down her face, back, breasts, and belly. "Fuck me. Cum in me. Cum in me! Alotta cum! Cum! Cum! Cumming – ooh, oooouuu, Shit! No! Can't!"

He pushed her out of the extended cab, boner dripping. He shook his head and walked back out to the salt water to wash the scent of Amris off of him. She did the same saying, "We leavin'?"

He nodded.

They dropped the wood chipper back off and left the Silverado for the contractors to use. They rode to the pre-fabricated houses by the lake and he entered the house. "Liza!" he called to her.

He went to the back and found it all cleaned up. Breakfast was cooking. He could smell the oatmeal, goat milk, honey, and raisins. Liza was in a terry cloth robe that she'd located in the closet. She looked at him.

"I woke up, you was gone," she complained in her girlish way. "Whatchu was doin'?"

"Sendin' Franco on his trip back to wherever," he told her as Amris came into the room. "He won't be here no more."

Liza hugged Amris. "Hey, Ami."

"Hey."

He hugged his wife and backed her into the wall, kissing her. She kissed him back at first then squirmed away from him when his hands found her naked torso and slipped inside to grab her asscheeks.

"Wait, Papi, the food." She walked into the kitchen and made three bowls of her "award-winning" oatmeal. Well, award-winning in *his* book anyway. He didn't know if it was the cinnamon, nutmeg, dash of vanilla or what but Liza knew how to put it together.

"What, you was walkin' by and seen Ami or – how'd this happen?" Liza used her spoon to ask, waving it between the two.

"Well, I seen him," Amris stated with a direct nod.

"What'd y'all do?" Liza asked.

"Liza, whattaya doin'? Leave her alone," he told her.

"They all ate."

"I like you, Ami, I do," Liza said when her man went back to the shower. "But I've been with him since he was ten. TEN. I know men love perfume, pussy, and paper. My man is a dog but he's a loyal dog. If I find out you trying anything behind my back, I'll *slit* your throat! You the type he'd fuck…and I'd let him. But if you bein' a greedy *poisonous* bitch, Ami, I'm *tellin' you.*"

He came back out with a towel wrapped around him. "You still fuckin' at it?!" he boomed at his wife, making her jump.

"Fuck you!" Liza snapped, standing up and blowing past him. "Where's my fuckin' clothes. I'm goin' home! You want her – *fuck* her!"

"Like Franco fucked you?!" he shot back.

Liza stopped dead in her tracks. "Whatchu say? What the fuck did you just say to me?"

Amris stood up to walk towards the door.

"Sit!" Sage shouted at Amris.

His wife was seething. "I'm leaving. I knew this shit would happen. Next, I'll be a slut, a T.H.O.T., and a hoe to you and everybody else cuz I let dude fuck me."

Liza got dressed. "I did it for both of us. I thought you'd liked it, too."

"I did," he admitted. "But I hated him after. I love you even more."

Liza wasn't breathing so hard now. "*What*? What am I missing?"

"Franco." He scratched at his ear. "He's gone. I chopped off his head while he stared at Ami in her yellow gym shorts. I set is all up. I wanted her pussy print there, barefooted, nipples pointing through her top."

Liza stood with her mouth gaping. "Dead? Right after?"

He nodded. "We took a contractor truck down to the end of

the beach, chopped him, fed 'em to da orcas, sharks, sea gulls, eels, and all that out there. I have his I.D., passports, everything. They'll never know he was ever in Monte Cristi."

"You fool, you asshole," Liza said with a smile on her lovely face as she walked up to him.

"I loved seein' my baby happy… but a mufucka gloating?" he said more than he asked.

Liza felt his raw power as he picked her up. She pulled his towel off and saw Amris stare at her man and how gorgeous his penis and body were. "You still wanna leave, Ami?" Liza asked the former black porn star.

Within minutes, Liza watched as Sage held Amris' legs draped over his arms in the missionary, hammering her pussy while Liza sucked her breasts. Speaking of breasts every time he looked at Liza, he saw all the bite marks left all over her body by Franco as she got fucked. The sight of them sent Sage into overdrive and he ended up fucking Amris so good that she had a wild squirting event that had her screaming.

It left Liza wondering negatively on one side. On the other, seeing her own titties in the mirror made her want to fuck another Franco because it made Sage so turned on. He even asked her the following day if him killing Franco angered her.

"Sage Michael '*Coldhearted*' Thomas," she started. "Don't think I'm bad but I never been more flattered or horny in my life!"

CHAPTER ELEVEN

El Gallo Loco

Santo Domingo/ Boca Chica, D.R.

1:00 AM Saturday

"That mufucka." Sage was pissed. "None of the homiez can find 'em?"

Tate shook his head. "We told him to lay low, keep the fizzam sizzafe but nobody's heard from none of them."

They were in Santo Domingo at one of Bienvenidos' Tiki Bars: *El Gallo Loco,* which was his most popular. An average bar in the U.S. usually can gross from $250k-$330k in alcohol sales alone in a city like Seattle, Boise, or Newark, Delaware.

There's most definitely a science to running a bar just like Jon Taffer of the *Bar Rescue* TV show can attest to.

No difference in the Dominican Republic. Carlos Juan Jaramillio-Garcia didn't make nearly as much for his bars but only because the D.R. economy was much smaller and much poorer. However, like anywhere else, the poor drank away their problems or used drugs to numb the pain that life brings. Carlos Juan was a millionaire and a well-respected businessman in the country by most people.

Not everyone. United States DEA and U.S. Customs agents were walking on eggshells in the D.R. whose government did not let them run amuck all over the island. It was no secret that American law enforcement knew that the Dominican Republic – this West Indies country on the eastern part of the island of Hispaniola – played an integral part in America's war on drugs. But since the inception of the so-called "cocaine explosion" in the mid to late 1970s, U.S. authorities were uncertain of the D.R.'s role, and anyone who knew the good ole United States of America (its federal government) they loved to point their goddamned fingers, assigning blamed and adjudging guilt on everyone except themselves.

For example, the 37th President of the United States from 1969 to 1974 was Richard Milhouse Nixon, (he was also VP 1953 TO 1961 under Dwight D. Eisenhower and lost an earlier presidential election to John F. Kennedy). It was well-known that to get elected he promised to increase U.S. military involvement in Southeast Asia – a promise he kept – where tens of thousands of black niggas and Latino niggas were sent to the frontline to die while fighting against millions of mufuckaz as brown as many blacks. They just have or had almond-shaped or "slanted" eyes. In other words, Asian niggas. Brown people.

Eventually, the Watergate building complex took place (1972) and after Congress recommended three articles of impeachment Nixon threw in the towel and resigned in 1974, taking his wife Thelma Catherine Ryan Nixon (AKA "Pat") with him. These points were made to highlight cocaine as *"the rich man's drug"* which made its White House debut when John Fitzgerald Kennedy was holding parties and letting Marilyn Monroe do what that stiff bitch Jackie Kennedy wouldn't do. Marilyn Monroe (AKA "Norma Jean Baker") from the movies *"Gentlemen Prefer Blondes"* and *"Some Like it Hot"* used alcohol, weed, and cocaine and JFK did, too. It's all in the news now how the Secret Service found cocaine in the lobby of the White House.

Sage, Tate, and Deuce were drinking beer and laughing following their conversation about Junior and his family being missing. That's all they knew at the moment. Liza came over with her poker face on, not wanting to talk about her father. At least not at the moment, the bar was packed. "Night-club/Restaurant" was more like it.

"Gotta be at least a thousand people here," Liza said as she took Sage's mixed drink out of his hand. "What are y'all laughing about?"

"America's drug war and cocaine in the White House," O.G. Bobby Tate stated, who was the Neighborhood Rollin' 60s Crip and her husband's "H.O.S. or head of security."

"Huhn?" Liza asked dumbfounded.

"Coke used to be the rich man's drug or the white man's drug," Tate told her. "At one time it was nothin'. It sat out in the open at parties, weddings, bar mitzvahs, especially in Hollywood. Richard Pryor used to come out of parties at Hugh Hefner's – the Playboy Mansion – and other celebs got autobiographies you just piece together history. Like Marilyn. Big tits, hips… JFK went nuts over her. She was a cokehead and so was half the West Wing."

"The U.S. authorities were wondering if the D.R. was growin' coca trees but they figured that one out easily," Sage added. "The land wouldn't yield street-grade coca plants. Not in this climate anyway. If it did, the *European* Spanish, in Spain, the Spaniards, would've known it."

The Dominican Republic had originally been inhabited by the Arawak Indians who were South American people vastly widespread through Colombia, Venezuela, Guiana, the Amazon basin of Paraguay, Brazil, Bolivia, Peru, and formerly most of the Greater Antilles. Also "Arawakan" was a large language family of South and Central America including Taino, and many other living extinct languages of South America spoken by the Garifuna. Most Arawak people today live chiefly in certain regions of Guiana. The D.R. had been claimed for Spain by Christopher Columbus in 1492 and it remained a "Spanish colony" until 1795 when it was ceded (surrendered via treaty) to France. "White History" when it favored them was all colorful and loud but when them bastards were given a black fuckin' eye, they didn't like talking about it.

The truth was that niggas got tired of the White Man's bullshit. There was a vicious and brutal uprising of slaves. Those Haitian niggas stood up and took swords, knives, and guns to white men, white women, and white children. The white children were slain so none of them mother fuckers could return to the island with hopes of exacting revenge on his father's killers. Haiti ruled The Dominican Republic after 1821. And then it became independent in 1844. But it had a very turbulent history which included over thirty years of dictatorship under Rafael Trujillo Molina from 1930-1961.

Times sure have changed. Cocaine was no longer the rich or white man's drug. The cocaine explosion had been replaced by the "crack-cocaine explosion" of the 1990's-present. Presidents weren't hosting parties with cocaine in the White House. However, NBC, CBS, ABC, or any of the big news media wanted to frame that cocaine was still found in the White House. "Lying Biden" had a cokehead son: Hunter Biden. Sage and Tate joked that he dropped it there.

"How's the food and the drinks?" Liza's father showed up at their table. He was an average sized man, very well-dressed in an all-white Valentino suit, burgundy gators, gold watch, diamond pinky ring, and gold bracelet.

Liza rolled her eyes but said nothing. The nightclub they were at *El Gallo Loco* was right behind The Catalina Hotel – D.R., and right behind El Gallo Loco was a boardwalk, located in Boca Chica which was still considered Santo Domingo. Liza was happy when Elizabeth, Noni, and Deva came down from their room at The Catalina.

"Elizabeth," Carlos Juan nodded at her.

She hugged him and they stepped off.

Liza walked over to listen to them talk.

"Give her that Carlito," Elizabeth was saying to her ex in Spanish. "You missed everything. She eloped."

"With him?" he asked her, indicating Sage.

"Mm hm," Elizabeth nodded.

"I saw La Hacienda De Helecha Negra being sold and I placed an offer that was denied," he frowned as he spoke. "Who had the capital to buy it? You?"

"Are you doin' the DNA test?" Elizabeth pleaded with him. "You're asking all the wrong questions."

"Why don't you come see me after closing?" he questioned with a sly grin.

Elizabeth was a chubby woman, her hair dyed red but her curves were everywhere men liked them to be. She did give in easily to him. She had told Lupé how bad she wanted sex and she wondered if Carlito could see through her act. Elizabeth had been lonely for a long time. She wasn't promiscuous at all. Her and Lupé were decent looking women and had no men in their lives. Of the two, Elizabeth had both young and older men eyeing her. So that's what she kept in mind when dealing with the man who Liza believed was her father.

Elizabeth removed the DNA collection swabs from her purse just as Liza appeared, quietly observing them. Sage and Tate were drinking a lot so she wanted to go to the hotel. Sage came up behind her, bent down, and kissed her right cheek. Sage watched Elizabeth.

"Tomorrow, bring everyone to Flora's," he said, covering Elizabeth's hand. "This is my business. Okay? Look, Liza, would you – do you need money? I can give you money. A car? I made mistakes not only with you but others. I never denied you… I -"

"No one's here for your money!" Liza scoffed and turned to leave.

He stared after her. "Okay give it, give it… what do I do? Do the damned DNA, Cabrón!" he cursed himself.

All Elizabeth did was swab the inside of his mouth with two different cotton swabs on long sticks. She put them safely into sealed packages.

"By the way Carlito," Lupé said to him. "You have a two year old granddaughter… and she's pregnant again with a son."

Bienvenidos stared after them as they went out. Sage was leaving a tip before he took off.

"Oyé, chico," Bienvenidos caught up with Sage.

"Wassup, Mr. Garcia?" Sage said. Tate and Deuce came back.

Bienvenidos checked all three of them out.

"I could be… I'm your father in-law then," the older man stated with great accented English.

"Whatever you say, man," Sage answered.

"Talk my daughter into comin' to Flora's tomorrow afternoon," he told Sage. "You got business in New York huhn."

Sage nodded.

"Flora's," he told him. "I have somethin' you'll want to see."

Sage and his men exited *El Gallo Loco.*

CHAPTER TWELVE

At least one dark secret
Catalina Hotel
Santo Domingo/Boca Chica D.R.

Lupé was sitting on the floor between Elizabeth's thick thighs while Elizabeth styled her ultra-black straight hair into a Pocahontas-style braid with an ornamental red silk flower on the left side. They were arguing or having a dispute inside of their hotel apartment.

"Boca Chica is Boca Chica, mamita. It's not considered Santo Domingo," Lupé told her sister. "You came to New York years and years before me. I was forced to pick up trash in the Santo Domingo slums with Tia Angela. We had to take a bus to Boca Chica. I remember because she used to remind me to lie about my age so I could ride free on her lap."

Elizabeth hit her with a comb. "That means nothing Lu. *Absolutemente nada.*"

Lupé elbowed her younger sister and Sage watched their interaction from across the room where she stood having a drink in the kitchen. There was a glassless window with a small countertop where anyone in the kitchen could see out into the luxurious living room and if they wanted she put food or beverages on the countertop. She was eyeing Elizabeth. Her demeanor had changed after seeing Bienvenidos.

"Whatcha thinkin' about, Pa?" Liza asked as she came into the kitchen dressed in white booty shorts with black horizontal lines.

"When I thought Tate was gonna fuck your mom but never did," Sage told her then grimaced right after saying it. "I didn't mean it like -"

"Don't apologize, honey. I know you're worried about her and that warms my heart," Liza said, kissing him.

"Look at both of them. They're so different in the D.R."

"It's home," Liza said. "Especially Lupé. See her brown skin?"

He nodded. "Now I understand. She's so at home here."

"You hit me one more time wit that comb, girl. I'll break raw eggs in your hair," Lupé cautioned Elizabeth as they continued to horse around.

Sage watched Elizabeth's small white teeth and gums as

she laughed. She had on a knee-length linen Dominican sundress which she had pulled up to mid-thigh as she did Lupé's hair. Lupé stood up and Sage couldn't believe it. He was most certainly checking out those big ass thighs he'd often snuck looks at and this time was no different except for one itsy bitsy fact.

Elizabeth was naked beneath the dress! And she wasn't all hairy down there like Sage had fantasized about before – in the past. He had probably thought that she was "hairy scary" but Sage loved hairy pussies. *Just don't start using a afro pick on that bitch is all I'm sayin'!* he wise-cracked in his mind while listening to one of those radio shows one day not long ago. It was one of the shows where the radio show jock asked the audience to answer the question: Do you like your significant other *"hairy scary"* or *"soft and bald"*? It was either D.L. Hugley/Mina-Say-What (WRNB) or Steve Harvey/Nephew Tommy.

Anyhow that wasn't even it. Sage was caught looking. Elizabeth didn't panic. She pulled the dress back down over her knees, picked up all of her hairstyling equipment, and exited the living room. *Damn!* Sage was saying in his head. Elizabeth had a pretty completely bald pussy, with the softest and loveliest thighs other than Liza.

It was 11:30 AM and it looked like Elizabeth and Lupé had decided to take Bienvenidos up on his invitation for them to meet him at his sister Flora's house in Oviedo, which was about a 90-minute drive southwest of the capital. Elizabeth entered Liza's room to talk to her about it but she was with Noni, Deva, Lilly, and Izzy getting their hair, nails, and feet done in Noni and Deva's suite on the same floor.

She ran into her son-in-law Sage, after he'd finished showering, shaving, and everything he had to do. He had on expensive Burberry denim shorts, no shirt, no socks, but at least his center was covered. She'd run into him before and understood why Liza screamed, shouted, and moaned so loudly. *She couldn't fake it with what that boy had!* She'd whispered to Lupé before. What she didn't tell Lupé about were all the times she'd pulled out the two dildos that were both black and measured in at 8 inches. One was slenderer than the other and it fit inside of her tight warm back door channel.

Everybody had at least one dark secret. Elizabeth did not always have to fantasize because what she thought about so often she lived with. She didn't have attraction for her daughter but she did envy the sex she had with her husband. At first, she abhorred Sage. The entire history with Daphne and how she died? She wanted to kill him herself. And then the way he had treated Maria and Papo – having them kidnapped and thrown out of his mansion in Mt. Vernon. Outrageous!

But that asset – along with the trust account he and Lilly had? Elizabeth and Lupé came from the dirt. Just like their family, Daphne and Maria. Elizabeth and Lupé – both who were trained midwives – had even plotted on poisoning Sage and killing him… but Liza had gotten pregnant with Izzy and things changed. Elizabeth and Lupé had moved in full-time with them. Elizabeth had seen and heard Sage in action with Liza. Sage had bulked up, he worked out, Elizabeth noticed all of the muscles and his raw power.

Rumor of "city's biggest drug kingpin" and "killer" only served to turn her on more. And, Elizabeth, being a woman in her late 30s…well, her blood ran as hot as any females on the planet. She may have been "overweight" or whatever but men loved meat on their women. Back in the 80s and 90s the "it" thing was "Big Butts." Before that blond hair big titties. Nowadays, women can be "small people" or a "small person" and she can get a NBA tall nigga if she wanted. Or Lizzo and be with a Pee Wee Herman mufucka. Black with white.

Just being a *woman* was in style. Size didn't matter because women had to do the real choosing. Elizabeth knew she had to keep it a secret what she was doing or feeling. She knew she should move out and get away but she was so attached to her daughter that it didn't come up. And as time went on, she heard the hot sex her daughter was having with her husband. Elizabeth tossed and turned in her bed. She would cup her hand over her pussy and apply pressure but that only worsened it.

"*Dios mio. Ayuda mi por favor, Señor,* (My God. Please help me, Lord.)," Liza's mother used to pray. But the only thing that helped ease the pressure in a pipe was release.

Once she started with the dildos she never turned back. The thicker one fucked her pussy and the slender one banged her asshole. And just when that orgasm hit her was when she would flip on the vibrators inside of each unit and… there was nothing or no one who was more delicious than that. Her self-induced orgasms would strangle her and leave her screaming and choking. Particularly when her G-spot would force streams of her female Bartholin gland cream to squirt from her like a human water main break.

"Lizabeth… *Lizabeth*," Sage said, knocking her out of her reverie.

"Yeah," she said. "Where's Liza and my grandbaby?"

He looked at Elizabeth. "You don't look like nobody's granny in that dress."

She smiled. "Stop it… *Really*?"

He put a Martin Lawrence smirk on his face. "Come on, Liz. You and I both know you got it poppin' off."

She looked at the full-length mirror. "You don't think I'm fat… and ugly?"

"You really believe that?" he asked her. "For real?"

She shrugged. "I don't know, Sage."

"I think you're beautiful," he said as he put on a pair of ankle socks. He came up behind her. "In your head, you see a fat woman when ain't a damn thing wrong with fat anyway but you... you ain't fat. You healthy and thick, like Liza. You have a perfect body to make a baby for yourself. You mad pretty. You clean. And smell good all the time… except when you blow da bathroom up."

She busts out laughing. "Uh uh! No I don't!"

"Seriously," he said, continuing on. "You have pretty feet, nice legs, and…"

He knew he'd better stop.

"And? And what?"

"Smooth thighs," he mentioned, his voice dropping an octave or two. "And I see you shave."

She was shy, looking at him in the mirror.

He came up closer behind her. "I know you haven't had a man in a long time… How long?"

"Long time," her voice croaked.

He slowly grabbed her right wrist and lightly toyed with her hand. "Liza thinks it'll be a big mistake to get tied up with Bienvenidos because you're so vulnerable. He almost destroyed you."

Her eyes were cast away now. "I've been lonely, Sage. And I mean *so lonely,* it hurts I'm so lonely."

"Don't let him have you again," Sage said, moving her long hair away from her right ear so he could talk sexily to her right there. He smelled her, her shampoo, her sweet Prada vanilla body spray.

"What will I do?" she asked lustfully, her nipples hardening on her D-cup breasts.

"What…" He took her hand. "…if… I…" He dropped his $450 denim Burberry shorts. "...found…" He wrapped her hand around his big hard cock. "…you… one… of… these?"

She turned, looked at him, then looked at his man hard throbbing, too, which she held in her right hand, but with her left hand, she slapped the shit out of him. He was just surprised that she never let go of his bone.

"That what you think of me?!" she hissed at him.

"Liza thinks that mufucka's gonna -"

"I know what Carlos will do, Sage!" she yelled at him, slapping him once more.

He backed her up against the dresser, stared at the flash in her eyes, and pulled her dress up. "I told you I'd help you! Ain't natural for no woman to go so long not gettin fucked!"

"Stop, you better not!" she told him.

He lifted her onto the dresser and she bussed open those thick thighs on her own. And he saw what looked like a baby oil leak because that's how wet and shiny her pussy lips were, her protruding clit and her small opening locked. He went down on that wet thing first and tasted her salty sweet musky juices. And she smelled fantastic.

"You got my dick ready to bust, Mommie, holy fuck… my shit is so fuckin' hard!" he exclaimed as he inhaled her wet, gooey flesh and when his tongue touched her clit, it *boinged*! Like a spring inside of a Bic pen or something. "C'mere!"

He pulled her up and into the bathroom they went. He locked the door to his and Liza's room and the door on the other side of the bathroom which was Elizabeth's room. They got naked on the floor and he gave her the best fucking she could ever remember having.

"You still going after Carlos?" he asked seductively, stirring that big hammer up inside of her belly.

She sobbed with pleasure, shaking her head. "I don't need 'em!"

He stared down at her, "Liza ever gon' find out?"

"No! No!" She vehemently shook her head, almost panic-like.

He grabbed her ass and waited for her orgasms to buss off for the second or third time. "This my pussy. I'm fuckin' you! Nobody else! Shit, shit, dammmmmnnnn… Lizzzzzz… you got that good coca, Mami!"

He spilled and spurted several nuts up inside of her. "Cum in me, Sage! Ooooouuu… so warm! Cum. Keep cumming."

Her pussy made that slurping, smacking, sticky noise until he slowed down and pulled out. He kissed her and hurriedly took a shower. Then he got dressed. He went to the living room and waited for Elizabeth. She came out minutes later and they were still alone.

"You good, Mommie?" he asked, checking out her new outfit. "You look laid back."

She smiled. "Shh, don't tell nobody. We'll still go but I don't need him."

"Thattagirl," Sage said, pleased.

Liza and everyone else came back in. "Mom, you goin'?"

"I'm goin' but not for that bastard," she replied.

Liza looked at Sage who was flipping through the channels on the large screen wall-mounted television. He just shrugged.

Liza smiled. "Ohhkay. *Bueno. Espera,* lemme get dressed."

"I'm comin' to watch," Sage started to get up.

"No!" Liza giggle. "We'll be even later."

"We flyin' or rollin'?"

"Helicopters on the soccer field across the street," Liza hollered back over her shoulders. "It's all arranged, Papi."

Thirty minutes later Elizabeth, Sage, Liza, Isabel, Lilly, Tate, Deuce, Spooky, Double J, Noni, Tate, Deva, Daniela, Lupé, and a dozen of their gunmen all boarded three black transport helicopters to take them to the resort city of Oviedo.

CHAPTER THIRTEEN

Ghostman Dinero
The Bienvenidos Estate
Oviedo, D.R. 2:30PM

Whereas when out of town or better yet "out of the country" thrill-seeking beach-goers wanted to hit the Dominican Republic and love the crowds and where all the action was, there's no doubt that they'd find it in the south. The southeast coast stretches for about forty miles or so and is dotted with the main beach resorts. Liza, Lupé, and Elizabeth took Sage, Lilly, and everyone else to Boca Chica, Punta Cana, La Romana, and

Santo Domingo. But, Liza told them about the Bayahibe fishing village turned beach and diving resort right across from Isla Saona that she wanted to take them to.

"Where we at now? I just see water!" Tate had to shout a little bit due to the noise of the low-flying helicopter.

"Look out there, y'all see the coast?" Liza pointed to her right. "Those are the cliffs of Barahona on the east-south-eastern coast of D.R. The pilots are flying in a straight point-to point so they don't have to be on land. They just cut across the water to Oviedo Lagoon and land right in Aunt Flora's front yard."

"This Aunt Flora… if she's your aunt, after the DNA I mean, well, wassup wit her?" Deuce, Tate's brown-skinned muscular nephew, asked. Deuce was the same age as Sage now, which was 18.

Liza pointed at her headphone unit. "I can hear y'all. Stop shouting…" they nodded. "There's no *if,* bro. Every time I come around him, I feel like I'm meetin' a part of me for the first time. Don't insinuate that he ain't my kids' grandfather cuz he is."

Sage heard their conversation. "Hm," was all he muttered.

"What motherfucker?" Liza shot at Sage.

"Don't blast at me, ma," Sage told her.

She rolled her eyes. "Bet $75k he my father."

"I'm takin' it that, he ain't," Sage said. "Only cuz I like to gamble."

"Bet," Tate also took the bet.

"Bet," Deuce said.

Double J elbowed his cousin. "Deuce, I just asked you for some cash so if you lose, please don't tell me no or else I'm fucked."

Sage looked at Double J. "Son, I saw the Savage Hoodz Records spreadsheets, download sales, and royalties and whatnot. You doin' the best."

Double J shrugged. "I need money, boss. Records are sellin' enough to pay everything else and everyone else but the debt I owe is killin' me, man."

"How much debt?" Sage asked.

"A rapper's dream is also his or her nightmare," Double J waved him off. "I'll handle it, big dog."

"Flora's Bienvenidos' dog," Lupé told everybody as they approached the shoreline. "She hides his money and... don't let her beauty fool you. She bites."

After landing on the helicopter pads - there were four with one helicopter already there - they waited for the blades to stop twirling to protect the women's hair. Then they got out and saw the lovely white Caribbean beach house mansion.

Tate looked at Sage who was shaking his head, saying, "This is what coke and heroin money buys ya homie."

"It ain't touchin' The Black Fern, baby," Tate told him.

The Black Fern was not a fancy modern Caribbean or Mediterranean style house but more of a Rocky Mountain or rich Montana residence. The Black Fern's primary house peered out across the Caribbean Sea through bountiful windows. Its natural stone façade gave away to a lodge-like interior with warm wood paneling and vaulted ceilings with heavy beams. The 13,250-square-footer comprised ten bedrooms and fourteen bathrooms, all with a rustic feel. Expansive indoor and outdoor gather areas with unobstructed views of the surrounding land and sea welcomed entertaining, though friends and family who visited may be tempted to steal away to the two 1,800-square-foot guest homes and kick back in the ranch cantina. Not happy with the current outbuildings that came with the place, Liza asked Sage if she could build a 6,000-foot carriage house with an enormous office, a full gym with enough machines to train a small rodeo team, and an underground wine cellar that could hold 3,000 bottles.

"It's a beach-front mansion. Y'all." Liza told them and explained that there were dozens of differences with the Flora Honoret-Garcia mansion and the Black Fern. "Ours is being built into a working ranch and bottling and canning fresh fruits and vegetables. And we'll dry fruits and package fresh fruits. So ours is a – or will be a – business with buildings and features for farmstead functioning. That's why we'll still need a 6,000-square-foot equipment barn, a 9,500-square-foot hay barn, a 2,240-square-foot horse barn, and a 4,000-sq-are foot equipment garage."

Sage let her grab his hand. "Long as you understand that we gotta go back to New York for all that."

"Papi, I said after our son's born," she quipped as they saw pink flamingos chilling inside of the small lake on the side of the enormous 15,000 square foot mansion.

"Babe, we spent way more than I thought we'd spend out here," Sage mentioned. "So, the equipment barn, the hay barn, a new horse barn, *and* a 4,000 square foot equipment garage? What the fuck is that?"

She implored, "You sayin' I'm spending up the ill-gotten cash... better I do it this way before the IRS takes it and our freedom."

"Well talk about it later. C'mon – that'cha aunt?" He indicated as they saw a beautiful woman around Elizabeth's age walk through two black doors that at first glance, appeared to be wooden but it was imported German steel.

"Liza? Come, Niña, come!" the well-dressed blond lady called to her and first embraced Lilly. Then she scooped up Isabel and kissed her chubby little cheeks. "Lupé and Liz!"

They all hugged her. They made all the introductions. Flora had very light brown eyes, she wore very expensive flowing dresses with bigger than life exotic flower patterns on them. Today, it was white with red and black rose designs on it, and it fell almost to her ankles. She hugged Liza and Sage at the same time.

"You two are in the Dominican news for buying the Black Fern place up north!" Flora beamed, looking at them. "You didn't know?!"

"Nope, did you know, Mami?" Sage asked. Liza only shook her head as they walked through the steel doors and into an indoor garden with a small fountain pool that had big hold fish swimming in it. There was a glass ceiling made of solar panels that must have cost a pretty penny.

Inside of the foyer floors gleamed with polished marble whose colors changed in every room. The mansion was massive and housed several generations of the Honoret-Garcia family.

There were armed guards everywhere at every entrance and on the roof. Bienvenidos showed up. He kept looking at Liza for over an hour before approaching her. Sage saw him and intervened.

"She good, Mr. Bienvenidos," Sage told him. "She's okay, sir."

"No. You back off and allow us to talk," the older gentleman stood firm. He glared at Sage.

"No arguing," Liza told them.

Sage shook his head. "This my wife. She is twenty years old now."

"I need to talk to my daughter," he said, catching the attention of Flora who sat across the family room on a long leather sofa.

"Daughter?" Sage repeated.

"Si, Señor. *Daughter,*" he said.

Liza picked up Isabel who was ripping past on her fat little legs. "Hm. Here. Start with your granddaughter," Liza told him.

He took the two and a half year old child and exhaled impatiently. "But…"

"Isabel Garcia-Thomas," Liza told him.

He held her out like an outfit while shopping at the mall. Isabel stared at him back.

"Abuelo, Izzy." Liza pointed. "Your Grand-Papi."

Izzy pointed at Sage. "Papi…" Then she pointed back to Bienvenidos. "Grand-Papi."

Bienvenidos broke out into a smile and moist eyes. "She's very smart."

"She's home-schooled already," Liza told him, and he hugged the little girl.

Moments later, they disappeared.

Sage whispered to Tate, "I thought comin' here was gon' be a party but it's some family drama shit."

Flora came over to where the men were hanging out. "You, they call you Coldhearted Sage, hm? For such a big warm man."

Liza eyed the woman who was supposed to be her aunt. She was fucking all the way stacked. Breasts 40 Double D, ass double the size but perfectly shaped like that sexy lady rapper Ice Spice. Flora had curves from shoulders to wrists and her walk was reserved for 40-plus women with that killer pussy.

Sage said to the woman, "Just Sage, Miss Flora."

Flora looked at all of the bodyguards so she ordered her security people to, "Take them to the shooting range."

Sage and all the other men went outside shooting to the

range while Liza, Daniela, and the other woman stayed inside the house to talk.

"That's what da fuck I'm talkin' bout," Tate said as they exited the main house.

The shooting range was an outside field with professional targets which was perfect for sniper targets. A dark-skinned guard for the Garcia's Oviedo estate set them up with some very beautiful weaponry.

Sage kept feeling his special Sat-phone ringing on vibration in the back pack he carried. He opened it and was told by Melissa Verducci, ESQ. - his long-time attorney - that they needed to speak.

He walked away from the loud sounds of the shooting that had begun. "You spot for Deuce, son, and then you, Deuce, be Tate's spotter," Sage told them.

"Is that gunfire?" Melissa asked.

"We're on a range, you on red phone, Lissa?" He inquired.

"Yeah, we – your hairline will move backwards once you hear who walked into my office today," she told him.

"Hm." He laughed in her ear. "If I gotta guess Imma reduce ya next retainer, Lissa. Who came to ya office goddammit."

"A man named… Adams," she told Sage. "Steven. Steven Adams. He left a file for you which has been forwarded to you. He took a swab. I did it myself and sent it directly out for testing."

Sage stared ahead as Liza came out to see the men shoot.

She saw his face and she immediately saw something moving inside of him. "Honey? What's wrong?" his wife asked.

He had so many questions. "Guess he's from Brownsville?"

"Fort Green." Melissa told him. "He went into the military days after he turned eighteen. He had pending charges stateside, but the military needed fighters in Afghanistan and just to…"

"Just to what?"

"Just to see him – *my Lord!*" she exclaimed and there was a short pause. "He's dark but very handsome… and he has a scary look to him. Certainly looks like your twin. Only that you're brown, he's black. Well, dark chocolate. I'm white… did that come out racist? Because you know how sensitive you Black Lives Matter folks are!"

"Fuck you, Melissa."

"Love you, too."

They ended the call.

Sage laid the contents of the call out as Daniela followed Liza and Lilly outside. Liza couldn't believe it. "Ain't it too coincidental?" she questioned him. "Bienvenidos first and then this Steven Adams person?"

Sage shrugged and read his father's military files out loud. "He names me in here. Oh shit. This my birth date and every-thing, mama."

"He got a moniker - a nickname," Liza pointed at the laptop screen.

Sage read it out loud, "Steven 'Ghostman Dinero' Adams. Hot damn."

"One more thing," Daniela said to the couple. "Don Bienvenidos in here says he'll make you a lucrative offer for The Black Fern property."

Liza shook her head. "Emphatically no."

"Huhn? You never heard the offer," Daniela said.

"Don't need to," Liza stated. "Save ya breath."

"Fifty million cash, fifty million product," Daniela told them and did a wash her hands gesture. "I passed the message. Don't shoot the messenger."

Liza's rage bubbled.

She was almost nose-to-nose with Daniela. "Bitch, you've worn out your fuckin' welcome. It's time you take your red-headed ass back to Calexico, California."

"Baby-"

"Don't *baby* me!" She yelled at him. Bienvenidos came outside. "This why you wanted me out here, you bastard?"

"No, I'd wanted that property long before it went up for sale, hija," her father said soothingly. "Forget it. If I would've known how upset you'd be -"

"It's my family's future, motherfucker!!" she snapped, not believing him. "I'm leaving..."

Liza picked up her baby, and then walked towards where the pilots were waiting. Suddenly, she stopped, and turned back to Bienvenidos. "Oh..." She took out her phone and sent a text to Aunt Flora and Bienvenidos while she stood with Izzy and Lilly only eight feet away. The text read as follows:

The red-head bitch staying with us in the daughter of billionaire Mexican drug baron Don Armadillio – The Bullet-proof Don, Flavio Mendez Santiago. The red bitch lives/travels incognito as Daniela Esmé Vallillo but real name is Flavia Naomi Santiago or La Colmillo so watch her. Her father, Flavio Mendez Santiago, supplies my husband with 50 keys coke, 50 of heroin, and he protects Daniela whose father bought VULKANYCKACYD.onion. She's a party bitch whose shared our bed and many, many others. If you want something worth more than my ranch better catch it before it flies south.

She hit "*SEND*" and smiled, a wicked glint in her brown eyes.

CHAPTER FOURTEEN

Lt. Blackstone & Scalese
Ossining, New York
Bronx, NY 2:00AM

L t. Claudia Blackstone and Cpl. Kendra Scalese of the WMDTF were woken up out of their sleep and they subsequently reported to the 46th precinct in the Bronx, New York City, at the behest of their captain who was at home asleep himself. At first, they had no idea why they would be ordered out of their jurisdiction to assist with a runaway child case.

"I shoulda been a bank robber," Kendra, a cute but

dangerous Jennifer Connely type, commented. She had very light freckles on her white Italian face, big pearly teeth, the green eyes to match Ms. Connely's, and raven hair cut to the shoulders and help up in a ponytail.

"A bank robber, why?" Blackstone wanted to hear this one.

"It's two in the mornin', Sarge, Jesus!"

"*Lieutenant*, dumbass."

"Exactly. Bank robbers make their own hours, in and out under three minutes and asleep at goddamn two a.m., man. For a child runaway case? New York has no social workers to handle these bratty kids?" Kendra complained but she was a damned good cop. Fortunately, Blackstone had the power to pick who she wanted to roll with.

"C'mon, Scalese," Blackstone told her as they turned onto Laconia Avenue across the street from Edenwald Projects in the Bronx. They parked right out front of the brick police station.

They got out of the car. Blackstone still had the black Camaro with the Stage II Yenko super-charged 1100 horse power engine in it. They went inside, signed in with the desk sergeant, and were taken back to meet with Detective Mark Humphrey. Inside of his office was a two-way window where they could look into another room. All it had in it was a table, wooden chair, and a steel bench. Sitting on the floor was a boy who was about ten years old wearing a gold sweat hood with blood on it and a pair of jeans with one tennis shoe.

"Little boy, about ten," the detective said. "One of our patrol units saw him J-walk right in front of his cruiser, covered in blood. We'd like to collect the clothes. But he was checked out at the hospital. They said he's in shock. He had this on him."

Kendra took the business card and showed it to Claudia. "Your card, L-T. How'd she get it?"

"He might talk to you," Detective Humphrey hoped with a short shrug. He got up to walk them to the door that led them inside the room.

"Did a body turn up?" Blackstone asked.

"Nothin' related to the little guy here," Humphrey replied. "We think maybe somethin' happened up in your neighborhood."

He put the key in the lock. "One more thing. He's missin' a shoe. One of my guys said it's a Yeezy shoe. Can you imagine that? Another reason why your Captain wanted you task force guys to investigate. This is a First Edition Yeezy classic – on a ten year old boy."

They walked inside the room, and Blackstone knew immediately who the kids were. "First off, c'mere honey," Blackstone extended her hand after she sat on the chair. She pointed at Detective Humphrey. "He called you a boy?"

"Imma *girl,*" she said in a small voice.

Blackstone showed the detective the little girl's bare left foot. "Toenail polish. Barbie toenail polish."

"My Lord." The man was embarrassed.

"This poor kid." Blackstone was sad. Very sad. But she had a job to do. "Did you run from somethin'? Where's ya Daddy and Mommy at?"

The child shrugged, scared.

"What's your name again, sweetheart?" the lieutenant asked her.

"Cassara," she answered.

"Look. How 'bout we take you and feed you and you can sleep at my house? I have a puppy and a kitten, and you can sleep with them. Okay?"

Cassara nodded.

"First, lemme have the sweat hood," Blackstone told her. "Whatever you have for her to wear lemme have it."

Humphrey brought her a sweatsuit and Nike boots that fit the girl who was not all that little. She had some muscle and fat weight on her. Blackstone knew that Junior had daughters and his sister, Delores, had daughters and Blackstone had Taizhan on deck as her snitch for the beef she got caught up in when the DEA bopped her in Corpus Christi. And since then, Taizhan has been telling Blackstone all the dirt. Firsthand, secondhand, whatever.

Blackstone wanted all the gossip on the street.

Flashing Back

Coldhearted stepped aside and let Junior in.

"It's – my fam in the car and -" Junior started, pointing a thumb over his shoulder. "I-I don't…"

"Ayo Junior!" C.H. stated firmly. "Don't come up here like you broken or a bitch."

"I ain't neither, cuz. Just tryna respect yo shit and Liza's!" Junior snapped angrily.

C.H. nodded. "More like it."

They walked together out to where Junior had his silver 2011 Tahoe parked and idling. Liza, Tate, Deuce, Kaz, Cumba, Ammo, and Daniela were standing around. Everyone knew that P-Man and at least a dozen of his goons had followed Junior from Garters Strip Club and caught Junior slippin'. That's how he'd got got.

"The Mercedes G-550 Squared," Ammo said to the huge man with a pistol whip gash above his right eye. "I don't see it."

"Err'body out," Junior ordered. He looked at Ammo. "Me and wifey was comin' outta Garters when we was jumped, hit over da head, and zip tied. Threw us in the back of da G-Wagon. They searched me and my address is on my crib in the B-X. They tied up my sister Delores; they see our apartment is full of our girls wit a slumber party."

"P-Man and nem followed yo blue G-550 squared wagon all da way from Garters to yo crib on Carpenter Avenue?" C.H. questioned Junior. "In the Bronx?"

Junior nodded. "Yep."

Junior's sister – Delores – was his complete opposite. Although she was slender, for some reason, she walked with a hunch in her back – as if she carried Junior's huge ass around on her shoulders all day.

"So they jacked the G-550, right?" Liza wonders aloud.

Junior nodded again. "That's right."

There were five eerily quiet young brown-skinned girls who stayed glued to their seats inside of the older model Chevrolet. Two of the girls – ages nine and ten – were the youngest daughters of Delores. The nine year old was name Ingram and the ten year old was named after Junior and Delores' mother who was no longer around. Her name was Betilda – Betti for short.

Junior's daughters were all bigger than they should be at their ages. Not "heavyset" and certainly not "overweight." Such terms at their new charter school were not allowed. "Bigger than she should be," was perfectly acceptable.

Junior's youngest baby was eleven. Her name was Cassarra. His baby in the middle was Jubilee, "Juby" for short. She was thirteen years old. And, last was his fifteen year old, Michelle.

BLACKSTONE AND TEMPORARY PARTNER SCALESE BATHED Cassara, fed her tater tots with hot cheese spread, a Happy Meal, and ice cream, and managed to pull it out of her that something bad had happened. They knew that Junior had a couple of homes. One in the Bronx and another in Mt. Vernon.

Search warrants were applied for both homes and the police found guns, taking cellphones, computers, records, and anything else they thought could be of some evidentiary value. Blackstone was a narcotics officer but there was something about this case that had "COCAINE" and "HEROIN" written all over it. She was given all the manpower she needed because not only was a tender age child found soaked in blood, but she had seen something so horrific that she couldn't get a sentence out without her teeth chattering as if she was freezing cold.

By 10:00 PM, Lieutenant Claudia Blackstone and her army of police, CSI, and Detectives had spoken to fifty individuals, including teachers from Cassara's school. She was sitting inside of her office when Scalese came in and saw Cassara crash out inside of a *Dora The Explorer* sleeping bag and pillow on the twin bed Scalese kept inside of her Mt. Vernon Police Department HQ office on the 4th floor.

"Your own money?" Scalese asked. Blackstone nodded. "Niiiccee. You like her."

"I give business cards to every kid I see and tell 'em it could mean five bucks, a meal, ice cream, or even a bike if they help me with somethin' big," Blackstone said. "We take plenty of money from the dopers. Fill out a 514 form – it's nothin'."

"Still no crime scene," Scalese mentioned.

"I'm afraid to find it," Blackstone stated honestly.

"I have a bad, bad feeling," Kendra Scalese shared with her boss. "I mean, what about all the missing persons we're hearin' about on the south side?"

"I thought about it. You think they're all linked?" Blackstone acknowledged, making a phone call to the Missing Persons unit. "Lieutenant Blackstone. You're on speaker with Corporal Kendra Scalese and myself."

"Tim Montgomery, what can I do for you L-T?" the officer asked.

"Tanya Taylor, Chubby Taylor, and all of those so-called Savage Hoodz Girlz and Boyz Gang that have come up missing such as Pearla Austin AKA Juicy P so on and so forth," Blackstone mentioned. "What has your department come up with?"

"Foul play," he said point blank. "We have some grainy video of a couple of suspicious men in a Water Works truck but that's it for the Taylor residence. Nothing on the others. I'm waiting for two cellphone records to come back... on Chubby and Sonja Jameson."

"These fuckers are good," Blackstone stated before she hung up.

A radio call went out citywide about a van that was being pulled out of the Hudson River. She perked way up and stared at Scalese with her mouth open. "What the -?" Claudia listened to the poor cop who was there to see what was inside of the van. Two words made the taskforce lieutenant jump out of her seat and snatch up her sidearm:

"*Multiple casualties*."

"Watch the kid!" Then she was gone.

CHAPTER FIFTEEN

"Vests on, gunz up"
Mt. Vernon. New York
4:00 PM

When Claudia reached the scene there were already two white coroner vans there. She telephoned Scalese. "We found our crime scene I guess. Four young ones, a woman I believe is Junior's sister Delores."

"The social service lady's here," Scalese told her boss. "What should I do?"

Claudia was right there, gloves on, looking at the bodies.

"Uhn, she isn't going anywhere with anybody. We're putting her in protective custody. It's already cleared."

Back in Mt. Vernon at headquarters Kendra Scalese was denying the social services worker access to the child. The woman was a light skinned black woman who was dressed very nicely and a white woman was with her.

"Must be an extremely bad thing that happened, huhn?" the black woman, Ramona Ari Brown, said as she waited for the elevator to take them back downstairs.

"It is," Kendra told them. "We're pulling her family out of the water now."

The white woman, Trisha Schultz, gasped and turned whiter. But she gathered herself and said, "Goodness. I hope she'll be okay."

After the women left Kendra idly wondered about them after they left. Those people could care less about the kids they stuck in foster care and group homes. They were resentful towards them and even hated them. But here was a white woman about to lose her dinner over hearing about bodies being pulled from the water.

A mile away from the police headquarters the social workers pulled into a service station for gas. A black luxury Suburban drove to the pump opposite from them and two men got out. Driving by the station was Cpl. Kendra Scalese and a bald-headed black male officer. Her hunch had paid off.

"Blackstone, you won't believe what we're lookin' at," she told the lieutenant. "I have an idea."

"Not with so many units," Claudia said after hearing her out. "These guys have more technology than us. Here's how we'll do it…"

Scalese had her eyes on Bugout and P-Man. The light skinned black woman who'd come in posing as a social worker was Seji Hooks, Taizhan's sister.

They were most likely plotting to kill Cassara because she was a witness. Junior was dead, too. His body was found about 100-yards north of where his family's bodies had been dumped. Claudia used a unit of seven cops to try and draw Bugout and P-Man out. She used Taizhan to tell a lie about seeing a female cop alone with Cassara at Kentucky Fried Chicken the next day.

"You'll get me killed, I swear you'll get me killed!" Taizhan complained about it.

"I swear I'll lock your ass up if you don't!" Claudia yelled at her. "This evening at 4:00 PM, it showtime."

SAGE KNEW THE BEST THING HE COULD DO WAS TO COME BACK to New York to close the deals on Garters Strip Club and his and Lilly's house. He left Liza alone with Amris, Vee, Blue, her mother Elizabeth, Lupé, and some others. Tate, Deuce, and the muscle he needed in his circle returned to New York with him. The first thing they did was turn back on the floodgate. Liza didn't get it but they needed the "spoiled rich bitch"

Daniela now. She kept the price low on the ye-yo and the diesel.

At his Garters Office Sage had to have an early morning meeting with Miss Verducci and the buyers from Atlanta. He walked away with $6.4 million after Verducci and the IRS got theirs. Then, he had movers package up the house and only $1 million he had stashed there.

"Y'all can sell SHZ records and make a big ass grip!" Sage told Tate and Deuce.

They were all at Sage's house.

"They said them niggas took out Junior's whole family, kids and err'thang," one of the Rollin 60 Crip homiez mentioned. "Junior, too."

That was one of the hittaz Tate had used to help him "clean up" shop when they took out Tanya, Chubb, and all the others. Mophead was his name. The "Mop" meant "mop up" but sleepers never realized that. Then there was Burn-Burn and B-Kode. They were all there.

"C'mon, let's go make our presence known, my niggas. Vests on. Gunz up," Sage shrugged. "I'm hungry anyway. Y'all want K.F.C.?"

"Hell yeah," Deuce stood up. "What about ya supposed to be pops though?"

Sage looked at Deuce. "You wanna pay for everybody shit?"

"Hell naw!" Deuce smiled.

Sage thought about him though.

CHAPTER SIXTEEN

Bugout holding MP-5
New Rochelle, New York
4:00 PM

T aizhan's heart, if it had legs, was about to leap and run away from her chest as she pressed dial on her cell phone. Claudia and her taskforce team of only seven officers stood around her as she called P-Man's phone.

"Ayo."

"Hey, Daddy. I see something I thought you'd want to see. A pics comin' now," she took a photo of Scalese sitting in the KFC on North Avenue with the undercover and Cassara.

A few seconds later he said, "Where's this at? On North Avenue, New Rochelle?"

"That's it," she said.

The cops used the little girl as bait then got her out of there.

"I'm fuckin' dead," Taizhan whispered.

"Get outta there," Blackstone told Taizhan.

"I'm dead anyway." Taizhan walked inside of the KFC and sat down.

Scalese yelled at Blackstone. "Hell with her! Take position!"

Blackstone ran into the KFC and tased Taizhan.

"Witness Protection stupid bitch!" Blackstone shouted as two undercover officers rushed in, grabbed Taizhan, and carried her back out to a car and drove her out of there. Behind the KFC counter were two undercover policemen, at the tables-sitting inside-were two female officers, both black.

"Subject one and two spotted, green BMW-four door, over," a voice transmitted over the police radio.

The police figured at that point that it would be an easy take down for outstanding federal and state warrants on the two men for RICO, murder, and a number of drug conspiracy felonies. The BMW paused to look inside of the KFC from the front exit.

Claudia was approaching after the car stopped as was her partner Scalese and the male cop who had taken Taizhan out of sight. However, they were all taken down by snipers with suppressors that P-Man and Bugout had positioned on the rooftops facing the front and rear of the KFC.

Claudia was hit but the shot had only cracked a rib and punched the air out of her lungs. Same with Scalese. The back door was compromised by the Damu niggas that P-Man had brought along. Inside, they found no Cassara, but they shot another officer in the belly and zip-tied the rest.

None of Bugout and P-Man's peoples saw Sage, Tate, and Deuce spot them on their way to the KFC. They sent out a group email for back up and made their move. "Take out them fuckin' snipers first, Mop and Burn. B-Kode, you get the one out back!" Sage commanded.

Tate pointed ahead. "Two… three cops down."

"Man oh fuckin' man," Deuce worried out loud. "Gon' be a thousand jakes over here in a minute and we gonna take blame for killin' cops?"

"I'm finna get these mufuckaz - who wit it?" Sage didn't wait for an answer.

He was only obstructed by some bushes out front of the KFC that was near the drive-thru but he could see Bugout holding an MP-5 and walking towards the down Claudia Blackstone, who was crawling towards her gun that had fallen when she got hit. Bugout raised his gun and Claudia held her hand out in a defensive posture.

"Don't! You don't have-" ***BOOOOOMMM!!***

Sounded like a Civil War cannon went off as Coldhearted

Sage Michael Thomas yelled, killing Bugout. "YEAH! PUSSY MUFUCKIN NIGGA! This -"

BRRAAATTT!!! BRRAAATTT!!!

Sage took two to the stomach, but he was Kevlar'd up! He dropped to one knee because his life depended on it! Tate and Deuce were battling it out at the front door with two of P-Man's Chicago Almighty B.P.S niggas. P-Man kept trying to tag Sage but he had him on the run around the luxury vehicle.

"Bitch ass Sixty niggas! Imma kill yo fuckin' ass!" P-Man shouted at Sage until his bullets ran dry.

"Put da gun down, fool!" Sage sat his gun on top of the car.

"Aight, let's do it, bitch nigga," P-Man told him. He put his automatic MP-5 down just as Tate and Deuce finished up out front. All the Neighborhood Gangsters were out full throttle-like "Sturgis Saloon" Mike and Angie Ballard.

They squatted up on the driver's side. But out of nowhere, Sage pulled a Walther PK 380. ***BOOOM!! BOOOM!!*** One to the neck. The other to the lung.

"It's a gunfight, ho ass nigga!!" Sage said in one of the most coldblooded and cool ways a nigga could.

There was a police radio on the ground that Sage picked up. He eyed Lieutenant Claudia Blackstone who caught a leg shot while all the lead was flying. Sage helped her up.

"Whatta we doin', boss?" Tate asked.

"Defense of a cop," he said, staring Claudia Blackstone in the eye. "Right, Lieutenant Blackstone?"

"That's what I saw. Scalese. Where's Kendra?" the Lieutenant asked, frightened for her team.

Gunshots were at a standstill. Sage asked Deuce, "We got any dead?"

"Three," he said.

"Get 'em outta here," Sage said as he carried Claudia to her car. "Neighborhood gotta get outta here. They know who we are. We're community business owners and we helped the good guys the papers will say."

Most of the Crips bounced. Tate told Blackstone, "Stay still, I was in the Army. Lemme tourniquet that leg."

"I'm sending the call out," Blackstone said. "Y'all coulda took us out. Finished us off."

Tate cut her pants and tied a tourniquet to stop the flow of blood, and he used her first aid kit to clean and bandage the wound. "You lucky it went clean through."

"You should both leave. Thank y'all for saving our lives," she said to them. "Go… they're coming."

Sage and Tate hugged like brothers because that's what they were turning out to be. They got the hell out of there and were glad that they were dealing with the type of female detective who had a name cats on the street both feared and respected. She played fair. Niggas saved her life so her thing was *I'd catch you later if you get caught slipping.*

Sage wasn't trying to be inside of *nobody's* jail cell. However, there was a whole lot on his mind such as the 800-pound elephant in the room…

Ghostman Dinero.

It was time to face the shit head-on. Especially, when Melissa Verducci texted him to call about the answer on the DNA swab Steven "Ghostman Dinero" Adams had taken. Like that alien-looking Maury Povich said so many times, "YOU ARE THE FATHER!"

Talking about having more questions than answers. The results of that test left Sage's mind *reeling. Fuck! What the fuck mom?! Arnesha. Steven Adams. Who the fuck am I? Is my Dad thorough? He a gangster? Fuck it. I know what to do.*

He facetimed his wife. *"He's my father, Liza! Steven Adams is my father, mama."*

Liza cried. He cried.

They cried together.

"He has to meetchu. And his grandbaby. So he can touch your belly, his grandson, okay?" he asked.

She nodded. "Grandsons. It's twins, Papi. I found out today. Look."

She showed him the ultra-sound photograph.

"They look like they in the pussy havin' fun cock-fightin' and shit. Hope they don't come out cupcakes!" he laughed, fucking around with her.

"So fuckin' stupid," she was laughing so hard.

"You know what this means, huh?"

Sage knew exactly what it meant.

"It means we goin' to Brooklyn where it all began for me," he said. "C'mon, ma. The house is sold. Garters sold. C'mon, you come get a fifty thousand dollar shoppin' spree. We get our cars out the storage and be out in the Bentley Continental GTC."

Liza booked the next private flight out.

They were so excited to meet Ghostman Dinero. However, by the time they would find out where he lived (he had a Chicago home and a New York home), word came back to them that he had been assassinated by his own mans. A crime boss nigga from Fort Greene named Joker Red.

PART II

Nature knows no indecencies, humans invent them.

-Mark Twain

CHAPTER SEVENTEEN

Stephen King Kinda madness
Brownsville, Brooklyn N.Y.
12:00 Noon

L iza, "Coldhearted" Sage Michael Thomas, who was holding little Isabel in his big muscular arms, and OG BOBBY TATE parked the obsidian clearcoat black S-580 Edition Maybach directly across the street from the 73rd Precinct of the New York Police Department in the notorious Brownsville section of Brooklyn, New York. The city had thought to finally build a multi-level parking lot for the area that had mostly been known for crime.

Rap and Hip Hop superstars Mash Out Posse (B.K.A.

"M.O.P.") were from Brownsville as was Mike Tyson – the best heavyweight boxer ever, hands down. Then there was Riddick Bowe, *"Brownsville's other boxer."* No matter where one went in the Five Boroughs they'd realized that as Queensbridge rap superstar MC Shan said, *"New York, a place where stars are born..."*

In the Summertime, there was nothing like visiting Pitkins Avenue to go shopping. There's nothing people can't find. Only a block or two over was the infamous Howard Projects. In the opposite direction was Dumont Avenue. That's where the Boriqueños and Dominicanos got it locked down. Then finally a little ways away on New Lots Avenue was Brookline Hospital. When a Brownsville resident thought about it... there's a bit of Stephen King kind of madness to hospitals that were next to the 'hood like Brookline Hospital or Kings County Hospital (Brooklyn was AKA Kings County).

Right up the street from Brookline Hospital were Noble Drew Ali Projects where AK-47s, 9 millimeters, Uzis, Mac-11's and AR-15s be going off like the washers and driers next to the Chinese restaurants on the 1st and 15th. The "Stephen King madness" was the beauty all out in the front of the hospital such as the flower beds, gardens, big picturesque windows, and the nice architecture of the building. While in the rear of the hospital that's where ambulances were rolling in the shot up, stabbed up, beaten down, near dead, the dead, and those who come to Brookline to die.

The madness and beauty of the 'hood.

The truth was in the back of the hospital, the beauty out front… was all a lie that delayed the inevitable.

They walked into the 73rd Precinct and Sage saw on the wall the photographs of police officers who had lost their lives in the line of duty. END OF WATCH they called it. Then there were these signs that had aphorisms and affirmations about the goals of the department. Dates the dead officer's service began, a little about them, and the "Mission Statement" of the NYPD to protect and serve the community.

"All the same bullshit that the worst kind of tyrant dictators said. They adopted it, polished up a letter, revised a word – but the same lying shameful deceitful bullshit." Sage stated and Liza thought he looked mad dope in his fly two-piece Saint Laurent black suit, white shirt, black silk tie and black Lebron's. He used to be a Michael Jordan fiend but when he heard that the former NBA mega superstar was investing in private American prisons that shit disturbed him. "Ceasar, to Stalin, Hitler, Mussolini, and maybe some others. But the more I read and research my eyes pop open more. Like I have more eye to see from and more ear to listen. These pigs is called pigs cuz of their appetite for destruction of Blacks. None of these photos in here got niggas like Eric Garner, George Floyd, Irizarry, and all the other muthafuckin' women, men, and kids who lost they goddamn life at the hands of a cop."

"Pigs is 'bout theyself," Deuce agreed. "Greedy, selfish fucks."

Tate nodded his head as Noni, Deva, and Lilly came in from outdoors. Deuce had driven the other luxury car that Liza and Sage had bought prior to the seven weeks they'd stayed in the Dominican Republic. Mop Head, Burn Burn, Spooky, and Double J were all chilling inside of the Escalade (that Liza and Sage used to own), keeping an eye on the $288K Maybach and the $229K Continental GTE Bentley. Although they had top insurance bumper to bumper on each car there was no way in hell that they were going to leave those cars unattended. They respected the Jux too much in Brownsville for that shit just like homeboyz book "*RESPECT The JUX*" had warned everyone to.

Their group had to walk through a metal detector, but they were all clean. There was a black staff Sergeant at the front desk who looked like a slightly smaller version of Dwayne "The Rock" Johnson with a full beard. Dude was super clean cut, smooth-shaven straight from Pops' Barbershop, ironed shirt, like he took great pride in the NYPD uniform. Sage saw the sharp creases going straight down the center of the triple stripes on the sleeves of his shirt. Sage had a wry smile on his face, flashing the brand-new gold and diamond grillz lacing the entire top and bottom rows of his mouth. *Either this ho nigga is a proud cop or he got a wife who irons his shit and hurries his dumb ass out the door so she can please her young hustla criminal lover the whole shift while her husband's at work. Likely the latter.*

"You finding something funny in here, young man?" the

NYPD Staff Sergeant asked in his well-known bad attitude and mean-faced growl.

"I do," Sage answered, not in the least hit intimidated by this big funky pig shit-smelling motherfucker. By nature, cops thought that they could push around, frighten, fuck with just any ole body with non-white skin, especially Black and Latino males and females no matter where in America their bitch asses were. Cops were always tryna harass Blacks. But more and more niggas were getting the courage and the spirit to stand up for their rights to protect police brutality and the racism that continued to permeate and persist among the ranks of white New-Nazi, KKK white cops who used racist ideologies to approach and lock up Black men and women. But today was a new day. The Black women and girls were bolder, they fight back like those 400-pound African lionesses did.

"You do, huh?" the black cop sitting behind the big counter replied. "And what's that?" he stated more than inquired, sensing something real dangerous about Sage. "Forget about it. Show ID and state your business."

Sage put his New York State driver's license down on the counter and the Sergeant called a female officer over. "Hey, Gayle?"

"Yeah, Sarge?" the white woman responded.

He handed over the driver's license to her. She took it and ran a check on Sage.

"I'd like to speak to a detective about this incident if possible." Sage took the tablet from Liza and the staff sergeant eyed Sage and his entourage.

"Press the square icon there so that the video-" Sage started, pointing.

He cut Sage off. "I'm not dumb, son. Hold your horses."

He pressed "*play*" and the video began to roll. There was the standoff, loud arguing and cursing…

Eight officers, one of them a Captain, a Lieutenant, and a female Detective First Grade, saw the Staff Sergeant watching a video of the NYPD in a standoff with a man some of them still remembered named *Titus "Big Kato" White*. He'd been a big guy who stood 6 feet 2 inches tall and 240 pounds. He had that real good hair, no hair on his face. Sage looked for any similarities between himself and Big Kato and there were none.

Except maybe his love for machetes. But that wasn't a genetic feature, Sage had merely adopted that dark part of Kato.

Flashing Back

THIS TIME, WHEN HE WAS RELEASED, THE STREETS WERE *laughing even harder behind his back because another man had emerged as a possible father for Sage. Now this ho not only fucked half the whole Brownsville but now Sage was "probably not" his son?*

The stick wets slurping sounds continued. **Glbb! Glbb! Mmm!** *The loud breathing and her sloppy sucking and moaning sounds had now filled the entire room. The candlelights seemed to burn brighter.* **Glbb! Glbb! Mmmm, Mmmm! SWWOOOSSSHHH!!** *A sound similar to a wire hanger slicing through the air at 100 M.P.H. And then, right behind that – a flat?* **TTHHUUMMPP!** *Sound. Something heavy hitting the floor behind the sofa. But Arnesha was currently throating her trick as if her life depended on it. She thought her son had dropped something and ignored it. All that mattered was the dick in her mouth and the $50 he had paid. She was trying to finish him off and get herself a fix.*

However, Arnesha felt the moisture of a misty-like spray hitting her face and forearm as if it were raining and a window was open nearby. Then, she realized that one second the trick's member was raging hard and then the next he was instantly flaccid. "What the hell, man?!" she complained.

She looked up at his face and she jumped backward, screaming as she fell onto her ass, knocking over the littered coffee table! The trick's entire head was missing!!

To her left stood Big Kato. He wielded a long, sharp machete in his right hand with blood leaking off the blade. Arnesha trembled and screamed bloody murder when she looked over to her right and saw the trick's head, it's eyes open, staring directly at her!

"OH MY FUCKIN GOD!!!" she yelled and then started screaming.

"Shut yo ho ass up!!" Kato boomed, pointing the machete down at her.

He turned to Sage and for an extended, silent moment he stared at him. Perhaps, he'd contemplated killing him. Kato had lost it. He had the look of a madman in his eyes.

"Every man needs his dignity, Sage," Kato declared to the boys. "Remember dat."

He used his cellphone to pull up YouTube. Once he was filming himself, he said, "Aight, duke, this must be how the White folks, school shooters, and terrorist do it, huh? Well, everybody, I just beheaded this dirty mufucka...as he was getting' head by a ho I thought I loved. Take a look..."

He showed the world the decapitated head as best as he could with the darkness in the room. ***"See? This is my machete, my kill. This is my... I think he's my son. This bitch is his mother - a whore. She fucked all of my boys, I'm a laughing stock. A man needs his fuckin' dignity. So this is how I'm goin' out."***

With that, he sat the phone down so it could record his next move. Then, he turned the machete on Arnehsa...

When the cops arrived, from the 73rd Precinct, he lunged at them with the machete raised in one hand while carrying

Sage with the other, as a human shield! He was cut down immediately with a burst of semi-automatic gunfire!

"Hold your fire!!" a yell came.

"Hold your fire!!" someone repeated.

"He has a child!!" an ESU Sergeant (Emergency Services or SWAT Unit) bellowed.

Cops discovered that the child had also been shot and that sent everyone into an even greater panic! Sage was rushed to the hospital!

But not even the YouTube video could have prepared them for the shock and horror of what was inside that apartment.

In huge bold black letters, the CSI Report began: *BLOOD... WAS... EVERYWHERE.* Like the title of a ROB ZOMBIE movie or something. Usually, this was something expected of a *crazy white motherfucker. Not a nigga in Brownsville, New York.*

Officers entered the station talking about the Maybach and Bentley Continental in the parking garage across the street, and the well-dressed men keeping an eye on them.

The Captain, who had stood by and watched the video, stepped up to the counter and looked at Sage. "I was on-scene about a decade and a half ago for that case. I'm Captain Brad Wannamaker. I'll be damn - you're the kid that was nearly killed back then!"

Sage nodded and the Captain came from around the counter and bulletproof glass.

"C'mon into my office," the Captain invited Sage and his crew. "I'll be damn."

They walked along a narrow hallway past a door that said: *Interrogation-1* and the *HOMICIDE SQUAD* and then they turned left. The Captain's office was at the end on the left.

"There's not a lot of seats," the White Captain said. "Is she your kid?"

"Yeah. Isabel. She's two and a half," Sage told him. Izzy looked up after hearing her name.

The Captain nodded and gave Isabel a small stuffed Koala bear which she beamed and accepted after Liza nodded okay. "To think, she almost wasn't here." A sobering thought.

It was a real but true, hard fact. Sage and Liza looked at each other, unable to fathom their baby girl not being here. A horrifying thought.

"Yeah…" Sage paused. "Liza's my wife, none of us in this room can't imagine a world without my baby. *Our* baby. I'd go crazy without her… or Liza."

"We're sorry, Mr. Thomas; the entire department is for what happened to you," the Captain offered but Sage was like: *now he wants to apologize? But you get more with sugar than with salt.*

Sage said out loud. "Thank you."

"Okay," Captain Wannamaker said, done with all the pleasantries. "Why're you here?"

"Steven Adams. They used to call him Ghostman Dinero,"

Sage mentioned, saying it slowly. "The case you're familiar with y'all prolly thought Big Kato was my dad."

The captain was on his computer and said, "Right. Titus White is now deceased. How do you know he's not?"

He gave the Captain a thin file that showed him the results of a DNA test done of a sample from Army Ranger Veteran Steven Adams. And there was a list of known associates known as "E.I.E." or "The Everything Is Everything" crew.

The Captain, curious about "E.I.E.", suddenly had a look of recognition in his eyes as he sent an email to someone in the FBI that he knew and, fortunately, got a quick answer. The Captain took a deep breath.

"Wow…" he said, shaking his head. "If this man was your father, he… *they* were some extremely bad people. The E.I.E. are suspected of one of Brooklyn's most notorious bombings. A murder case involving over a dozen Italian Mafia. The leader is David 'Joker Red' Hodges. If Ghostman Adams was executed, Mr. Thomas, it had to happen with the boss's say so. Joker Red leads a crew so powerful that they were able to make our investigation go away."

Tate, Liza, and everyone else's ears perked up.

"Goddamn," Tate murmured.

"You know this how?" Sage asked.

"FBI and ATF investigators," he told them. "An email here, another there. We have open lines of communications. Our East New York guys were on that case but we were all assisting because it was such a big deal. And it wasn't that long ago that a friend – Detective Genovese – was killed, and the rumor is that Joker Red's new ally, Don Frank Braga, asked Joker Red to use his people to do it."

A NYPD cop killing is a huge deal. It also sounded familiar. It was all over the news. The "1-800-COP-SHOT" phone number derived from the murder of a cop named Edward Byrnes in Queens as he sat outside of a state's witness' house. Along with the 1-800-COP-SHOT number for any shooting death of New York City Police the City offers $25,000.

"O'Mira Dukes, cousin and business owner," the Captain told them. "Westchester County… New Rochelle we have. Joker Red, we think, murdered his own cousin, Skeet Dukes, but we cannot prove it. That's all I can help you with. I shouldn't have given you that much."

Sage shrugged. "Then why did you?"

"I feel I owe you one from when one or more of us nearly killin' you a long time ago," the tall man with the protruding belly stated. "Not that it absolves me of the mistake," this time, *he* shrugged. "But you have to seek forgiveness wherever you can. Nothin' wrong with being sorry for a wrong you did."

They started to leave. Sage asked the Captain, "You have a wife and kids?"

The captain looked at a framed photograph on his desk. "Even got a grandson now."

"Give the Captain a taste, Mami," Sage told Liza.

She placed a stack of cash on top of his desk.

"Burn it up, baby," he further instructed her.

Liza placed a new fully charged cellphone next to the $3000 cash. A burner. Hence, "burn it up."

The Captain stared at Sage for a second. "Mr. Thomas, since you walked in, we scanned and facial recognized your whole group. My Lieutenant sent me several emails from Mt. Vernon and Bronx detective squads on who you've become. You're a bad guy, the leader of an army of Rollin' 60 Neighborhood Crips."

"Leader? I'm no fuckin' leader," Sage protested. "Imma businessman."

"Shut up!" The Captain got in his face, but he put the cash and the phone into his pocket. "You shut up and you listen. All you assholes listen. You're *young* and you're *stupid* but personally, I been waiting for a fuckin' *real* bad guy to materialize and go against this fuckin' Joker Red and E.I.E. mercenaries. They're a legit Private Military Corporation."

Tate's ears perked up. "*Mercenaries,*" he repeated. "That what they really are or what they call themselves?"

The Captain was frank. "Youse don't understand what you're walking into. Google The Villa Strip Club Massacre and educate yourselves on PMCs."

Liza, Tate, Deuce, and every one of them in the group Googled the infamous nightclub massacre and instantly found links to the videos related to it. And the Good Private Military "Corporation" or "Company" or "Contractor."

"*That's* who murdered your Father," Wannamaker said

after they saw the videos. "I have the burna. Don't do any pokin' around. The guys and you'll have two dozen military trained killers at your door. And by *trained*… I heard they put fear inside of ISIS and Al Qaeda guys."

"Because of that Brooklyn bombing massacre… I saw the burned bodies…" he shook his head and scratched his chin. "Then Hanna's being murdered… I regret tellin' you about O'Mira Dukes because youse aren't ready for these guys."

"Imma thinker, Cap," Sage assured him. "And I happen to know a guy who was in the U.S. Army that just might be able to get us into Joker Red's PMC. Are you a real enemy of that dude? That's the fuckin' issue."

"Once I answer that, I've crossed a line," the Captain realized.

Sage nodded. "Ain't no rats in my family. If there were you'd know it anyway."

"He's our enemy, Thomas," the cop said assuredly. "At Genovese's funeral there was sadness… but there were hundreds of the angriest bastards I've ever seen. In our Precinct, you punch one of us you get a beatin'… but to take out one of our Detectives? When you get arrested… *'oh he reached for my gun.'* You're dead. You won't make it to court."

Sage believed him. "The phone is *RedPhone* ready and *Textsecure* ready."

"Darknet encryption. I know about it," Wannamaker said. Sage and his peoples left.

"Wow," Tate said. "You feel comfortable with that dude?"

"Cold comfort," Sage said, calling for the cars to be brought to them at Soxby's Bar & Grill on the corner up the street from the 73rd Precinct.

"But from what he told us, this Joker nigga's fuckin' damn near untouchable. But just like we used the cops to bury them Blood niggas…"

"Nigga that was *luck,*" Deuce reminded him.

When the shootout at the KFC went down the task force never had the appropriate manpower to take down Bugout and P-Man who didn't realize until it was too late that they'd been played by Taizhan who set them up for a task force ambush. If not for how bad Sage and the Rollin 60s wanted the Almighty Black P. Stone leadership dead, Blackstone and her deputies would've been cooked.

"Yeah, well," Sage stated as they ordered beer and steak dinners. "NYPD, our enemy hates my enemy, and I can use that to my advantage."

Mophead, Burn Burn, Spooky, and Double J joined them after leaving the Escalade, the Bentley, and Maybach in the parking lot.

"I was hungry as hell," Burn Burn said as a waitress pulled a table over to the booth. "Don't break a sweat, pretty brown thang, we got this. Shiid, matter fact, you should join us!"

The black girl giggled, all her teeth flashing at the compliment. She stood to the side while Mop, Spook, and Double J looked at her bubble booty in the cute white nylon pants she wore.

"What's the move?" Spooky inquired after the waitress exited.

"Wait 'til we get to the hotel," Sage told everyone. "Too many ears."

They had a great meal before leaving.

CHAPTER EIGHTEEN

"Today I choose love"
The Plaza Hotel, Manhattan
11:00 AM

They stayed at The Plaza in Manhattan. Liza wanted to return to the Dominican Republic since there would be no meeting of Steven "Ghostman" Adams. Sage was so salty that she wanted to leave right away.

"What are *you* gettin' mad for?" she asked. "The logical thing is that you have a wife and twins on the way. Get to the D.R. and care for *them.*"

"You really think Ima let this mufucka live and he

murdered one of mine?" he shouted. "On top of that, you said you needed all this extra shit out there for the land and the business?"

"Forget it," she said. "We don't need it. Just – let's go!"

"Babe, I wired the money from the house sale for The Black Fern," he told her. "It's out there for you to use. Just go to our bank. The rest, I have to bust a move for the Rollin 60s."

"Imma be by myself!" she protested wildly as he stood by the mouth of the living room area of their suite where the team was hanging at.

"You *choosin'* that. Plus ya moms and nem are out there wit all da guns I got in place," he pointed out. "Then Amris and nem."

She smacked her teeth. "I ain't tryna hear you, man. I'm pregnant and you in fuckin' America while I'm in the D.R. How you sound?"

"I can be arguin' jus' as loud and hard for you to stay and lemme make this twenty-five million but I'm not tryna stress you," he said in a begging voice. "But I got a task force lieutenant up Westchester who owes me her life and a Brooklyn NYPD Captain on *RedPhone* speed dial."

She walked into the bathroom in some new pink velour Jordan jogging pants, pulled all up in that insane ass and asscrack, and he knew he was about to fuck her and suck her.

He kicked everybody out of the suite and told them to go to Noni and Deva's suite while he finished talking to his wife.

"Take Izzy, Dev," Sage said.

"Liza bout to get her pussy stretched out," Noni laughed and Sage locked the door.

"What?" Liza snapped at him. "Go fuck that Lieutenant bitch. Don't even try it wit me, punk bitch."

Sage snatched the hairbrush from her and she slapped him. He lifted her up and carried her to the bed, deep French kissing her sexy ass. He stripped, then stripped her.

He went to her neck, biting and sucking all on her titties. Her nipples stood straight up. "This whatchu really want, ain't it?"

She nodded. "Oh my god, Papi, I need you."

To her belly which was getting bigger now. And he bent her knees back and smelled her musky, turned-on aroma. The twin pregnancy made her secretions tastier and thicker and that made him harder, more aroused.

She pulled him up to her and licked her cunt nectar off of his fine ass lips. He saw her smelling herself on his chin and upper lip and he found it sexy.

"You smell and taste different," he informed her.

She nodded and whimpered because the large brown cucumber battering ram was sinking deep inside of her sweet pink depths. "You make me change. Your two babies. You like it?"

He was deep stroking her good young pussy. "Hell yeah, Mommy. I love you and don't want you to leave me. Don't leave me."

She hugged him. "I won't, Daddy. Ooh, fuck me with my long, thick dick! Touch our babies, Daddy!"

He made sure not to fuck her. He made love to her. Even when he turned her onto all fours and licked her pink anus before easing inside of her, he squeezed her softly.

"I love you, Liza, you my heart, Mami." She took that huge banger slow, and she came in hard gushes of pungent pussy cream. "Come back. Gimme my pussy."

She got back in the missionary position, and she gave it up until all of that sloppy wet squirting started all over the place. As she orgasmed, he squeezed her ass, and she screamed while biting his shoulder and neck.

"Open 'em!" he demanded. "Gimme… that… fuckin'… pussy! C-cuuumm-iiii-nnnnnn' ohhh, Mamiiii!!"

He shot that hot river of semen all inside of her. She gyrated her sweaty torso all into his. ***Squish! Slap! Squish! Slap! Squish! Slap!*** Sounds of steamy sex mixed with the oohs, aahs, and everything else.

She pulled the covers up over them before they got too cool. "I love you, Daddy. I mean my heart cries to leave your side when I don't know – if I'll see you."

He nodded, stroking her hair. "Me, too."

They were both emotional.

He kissed her and held her tight. "You're my wife and I love nothin' more than you, Izzy, and Lilly."

"Not even revenge?" she asked him, laying on his chest.

"Today, I choose love, Mama," he promised. "Today, I choose my woman and children."

She didn't know what it was about what he said but Liza cried.

She smiled, crying happy tears.

The End

REVIEW

Did you enjoy the read?

Let us know how much by leaving us a review on Amazon
and Goodreads

OTHER BOOKS BY

URBAN AINT DEAD

Tales 4rm Da Dale

The Hottest Summer Ever

Hittin' Licks For The Holidays: Atlanta

Wet Dreams On Lockdown: The Nurse

How To Publish A Book From Prison

By **Elijah R. Freeman**

Despite The Odds

By **Juhnell Morgan**

Good Girls Gone Rogue

Good Girls Gone Rouge 2

By **Manny Black**

Hittaz

Hittaz 2

Hittaz 3

Hittaz 4

Hittaz 5

Coldhearted

Coldhearted 2

By **Lou Garden Price, Sr.**

Charge It To The Game

Charge It To The Game 2

A Summer To Remember With My Hitta

Snatched Up By A Hitta

Santa Sent Me A Real One For Christmas

Wet Dreams on Lockdown: The Unit Manager

Thug Me The Right Way 2

Thug Me The Right Way 3

Seizing A Gangsta's Heart For The Summer

Yours For The Taking

By **Nai**

A Setup For Revenge

A Setup For Revenge 2

Wet Dreams On Lockdown: The Librarian

By **Ashley Williams**

Ridin' For You

Ridin' For You, Too

Trickin' on a Heaux for Christmas: A BBW Love Story

Homie Hoppin' For The Holidays

Wet Dreams on Lockdown: The Female C.O

Letters Of His Love

By **Telia Teanna**

The State's Witness

The State's Witness 2

The State's Witness 3

This Time Won't You Save Me

This Time Won't You Save Me 2

His Summer Side Piece

By **Kyiris Ashley**

Stuck In The Trenches

Stuck In The Trenches 2

By **Huff Tha Great**

The Swipe

The Swipe 2

By **Toōla**

Melted the Heart of a Menace

Wet Dreams On Lockdown: Lieutenant Grace

By P. Wise

Merry Trapmas: Ice & Frost

By **Mia Sky**

Thug Me The Right Way

By **DiamondATL & Nai**

Atlantastan

Atlantastan 2

By **Chris Green**

IN The Streetz

IN The Streetz 2

IN The Streetz 3

By **Tron Hill**

Wet Dreams on Lockdown: The Male C.O

By **Tamyra Griffin**

Wet Dreams On Lockdown: The Counselor

By **Paris Iman**

Wet Dreams On Lockdown: The Warden

By **Shawnice**

Wet Dreams On Lockdown: The Captain

By **TN Jones**

Coming Soon From
<u>URBAN AINT DEAD</u>

The Hottest Summer Ever 2
THE G-CODE
Tales 4rm Da Dale 2
How To Invest In The Stock Market From Prison
By **Elijah R. Freeman**

Hittaz 6
By **Lou Garden Price, Sr.**

The Swipe 3
By **Toola**

Good Girls Gone Rogue 3
By **Manny Black**

Despite The Odds 2
Hittin' Licks For The Holidays: Chicago
By **Juhnell Morgan**

Charge It To The Game 3
By **Nai**

Ridin' Foreva

BOOKS BY

URBAN AINT DEAD's C.E.O

<u>Elijah R. Freeman</u>

Triggadale

Triggadale 2

Triggadale 3

Tales 4rm Da Dale

The Hottest Summer Ever

Murda Was The Case

Murda Was The Case 2

Murda Was The Case 3

Hittin' Licks For The Holidays: Atlanta

Wet Dreams On Lockdown: The Nurse

How To Publish A Book From Prison

9 798990 674851